The Timothy Diary

The Timothy DIARY

GENE EDWARDS

SeedSowers Publishing
Jacksonville, Florida

Visit SeedSowers exciting Website at www.seedsowers.com

Library of Congress Cataloging-in-Publication Data

Edwards, Gene
The Timothy Diary / Gene Edwards
p. cm. - (First-Century Diaries)
ISBN 0-940232-95-2
1. Timothy, Saint -Fiction. 2. Church history - Primitive and early church, ca. 30-600-Fiction. 3. Bible. N.T.-History of Biblical events-Fiction. I. Title.

To the brothers and sisters
Who gather in Jacksonville, Florida
Jacksonville, my Ephesus

BOOKS BY GENE EDWARDS

In a Class by Itself
The Divine Romance

Introduction to the Deeper Christian Life
Living by the Highest Life
The Secret to the Christian Life
The Inward Journey

Books on Inner Healing
A Tale of Three Kings
The Prisoner in the Third Cell
Letters to a Devastated Christian
Climb the Highest Mountain
Exquisite Agony
(formerly titled Crucified by Christians)
Dear Lillian

Radical Books for Radical Christians
Overlooked Christianity
Rethinking Elders
Revolution: The Story of the Early Church
How to Meet in Homes
Beyond Radical

The First-Century Diaries
The Silas Diary
The Titus Diary
The Timothy Diary
The Priscilla Diary
The Gaius Diary

The Chronicles of the Door
The Beginning
The Escape
The Birth
The Triumph
The Return

PROLOGUE

I am Timothy of Lystra.

Word has reached me that my dearest friend, Titus of Antioch, is dead—executed by Roman soldiers. He met his death on the Isle of Crete.

It is on this day that I shall begin to fulfill a promise I made to Titus. That promise was to continue the story of Paul's journeys. (I shall begin where Titus left off.) What you are about to read, then, is the record of Paul's journey to Ephesus.

This journey, Paul's third, was quite different from his first two. This journey was the fulfillment of Paul's dream, since it was in Ephesus that he trained a handful of men to take his place.

By recounting to you this journey of journeys I not only fulfill a promise I made to my friend Titus, but I also leave you with an understanding of how Paul trained those men to plant churches. I take delight in doing so for many reasons, but certainly one reason is that you will know the role Titus played in this great saga.

Titus ended his part of the story—Paul's *second* journey—at the point where Paul and I were about to enter Jerusalem to celebrate the Passover Feast. Titus chose an excellent place to close his part of the story, and I will take up exactly where Titus left off.

Come now with me to Jerusalem, where an excited young man is about to pass through the gates and enter Jerusalem. This simple act turned out to be a little more complicated than I expected.

CHAPTER 1

"Timothy, the gates of Jerusalem! Pass through them and enter the Holy City."

And so we did. But Paul's next words were, to say the least, a surprise. "You must not wander these streets. It is not safe for you to be in Jerusalem."

"Why?" I questioned in utter surprise.

"You look like a Greek. That is why," replied Paul. "You are, in fact, the most Greek-looking Greek I have ever laid eyes on. Consequently, you are in danger. The closer you move toward the Temple, the greater your danger. These are not normal times in Jerusalem. There is murderous antagonism toward Gentiles, especially during festivals, and more especially *this* festival."

"But I am a Jew. A circumcised Jew," I protested. "You know I am a circumcised Jew. It was by your hand I was circumcised. I have a right to enter the Temple," I added testily.

"And as you enter the Temple ground, can you *prove* that you are circumcised?"

"Uh, no—but I am."

"You may be a Gentile attempting to sneak into the Temple. And at this particular time in Israel *that* would be *very* dangerous."

"Even if I am with *you?*"

"With me? With Paul of Tarsus? If you were the most Jewish-looking Hebrew since Abraham, you would be in danger *because* you were with me."

"Are you telling me I came all this way from Corinth, Greece, and I will not be able to see the Temple?"

"There is a way. I will tell you how. Right now, however, I must go to the Temple altar, where I will bring to completion the vow I made in the synagogue in Cenchrea. I will go to the altar, repeat my vow, and then throw the hair shaved from my head into the altar fire." Paul smiled. "Unless the Daggermen are after me (and can recognize me in my bald disguise), you can be sure that a bald-headed man throwing hair into the altar's fire will be accepted as being Hebrew. As for you and your Greek face, we *do* have provisions for Jews who do not look like Jews."

"You better have," I replied impatiently.

"Here is what you must do. You must appear before a tribunal of priests. There you must prove you are a Jew."

"How?"

"The priests have their ways," replied Paul, who was obviously relishing my frustrations. "You will be asked many questions. Be sure, the priest who inquires of you will be very skeptical of any and all of your answers. Further, you will be *inspected.*"

"Oh no!" I protested again.

"Look at it this way—when you get to Antioch you will meet Titus. There the two of you can exchange stories about your being inspected.

"When you have finished the inquisition, *if* the priests approve you—which I doubt—meet me at the eastern gate that goes into the Temple courtyard. But if you fail to be approved, do not venture anywhere near the Temple grounds. Instead, return *here*. Without priestly approval, you must not go into the city. Not until the Passover celebration is over."

"You are not going to tell me anything more than this, are you, Paul of Tarsus? Can you not at least tell me some of the questions they will ask?" I hesitated. "And maybe some answers?"

Paul laughed. "Let us hope Eunice and Lois have taught you well. If not, you will miss out on the festival. This is all you need to know. Now I must complete my vow. I will meet you either at the eastern gate or here. Whether you observe the festival or not will be decided by the priests. This is our way. Be a good Hebrew and yield to our Jewish customs."

"What are the chances I will fail?"

"They are not too great, not if you are really a Jew," laughed Paul.

Having said that, Paul moved toward the Temple. Hesitantly, I followed Paul's instructions on finding the priests who would decide my Jewish fate.

At that moment, unknown to me, both Paul and I were in very real *danger*, but Paul far more than I.

The Daggermen *were* looking for Paul at that very moment. Not to kill him, but simply to see what he looked like so that they might recognize him again *if*, on some future day, they decided to assassinate him. But the Lord was merciful. During our entire stay in Jerusalem the Daggermen never once saw Paul. He could thank his shaved head for that. With a head *that* bald, even close friends would not have recognized him.

I, in turn, had the opposite problem. From the angry stares I received, I knew that I was quite easy to identify. *Everyone* thought me to be a heathen Gentile. Tensions in Israel were high, and no Jew wanted a Gentile around trying to disguise himself as a Jew so as to participate in a Jewish festival.

By the time I reached the appointed place, I was more than ready to leave the city. Anger toward me was evident everywhere. Furthermore, I had *no* idea how difficult it would be to *prove* I was Jewish. But I soon found out.

CHAPTER 2

"You are not a Jew. You are a Gentile posing as a Jew so that you may slip into the Temple and learn the secrets of our customs."

"No! I am a Jew."

The priest eyed me skeptically.

"No, you are a Gentile. A Greek. I know. I do this at every festival. I am very good at identifying Gentiles, and *you* are a Gentile. In fact, you are the most Greek-looking Greek I have ever seen."

"You are not the first to tell me this," I sighed. "But sir," I continued, trying to remain calm and at the same time be convincing, "I *am* a Jew. Circumcised by a Jew. A Pharisee circumcised me."

"Your father was a Jew and your mother a heathen!" he exclaimed. (Were that true, I would be disqualified from Judaism.)

"No, my mother *is* a Jew. My father was a heath . . . uh, a Greek."

"Tell me the law," he demanded.

"The Ten Commandments or the whole law?"

"You know all 620 laws, rules, and ordinances?"

"Well, no. I usually forget one or two."

"So do I," responded the priest, lowering his skepticism a little for the first time.

"Tell me of Abraham!" he said gruffly.

The answer I gave was not a wise one.

"Abraham was a *heathen Gentile* the day he was justified. He was justified *before* circumcision and a Jew *after* circumcision."

"Enough of that!" barked the priest. "Tell me of your mother."

I recited my mother's genealogy back fourteen generations. *This*, at last, seemed to placate my interrogator.

"How far from his home may a Jew walk on the Sabbath without breaking the Sabbath?" he demanded.

Again, I was unwise in what I said.

"Not far! But if he is a religious legalist, playing with the will of God, he can sit down on the road, eat some bread and water, claim *that* place to be his home, rise up, and walk again. He can do this all day long, but I doubt he has kept the Sabbath."

To my surprise, the priest laughed. "You will never make a good Pharisee! Define the Sabbath," he jabbed, regaining his stern demeanor.

"God is our Sabbath; the day of rest is but a picture of him."

"Your mother taught you this?"

"No, the Lord did."

The priest stared at me, then began pelting me with questions I *knew* he did not usually ask. Many answers I did not know; some I did. We even got into an argument (which convinced me I had been approved)!

Finally he asked, "Who circumcised you, young man?"

"A man named Saul."

"A Pharisee?"

"Yes."

"Possibly from Tarsus?"

"Have you any right to ask that question?"

"I suppose not, but if it is Saul of Tarsus, there are those who would be surprised that *he* circumcised *anyone.*"

"Circumcision is circumcision!" I replied. "No matter from whose hand it comes."

"You know too much," grumbled the priest.

"I am approved?"

"Yes, but one last question, Timothy of Galatia. Do you believe the Messiah has come?"

"Yes! And he was crucified in this city twenty-four years ago. In fact, twenty-four years ago as of *tomorrow!*"

"Hmmm," replied the priest, "I sometimes believe the same."

"Here," he said finally. "Put this around your neck. It is the *chain of approval.* But be very careful. Wear the chain in plain sight. Never let your clothes cover any part of it. Especially when you are in or near the Temple."

"Why?" I asked.

"Why? You do not know? Because if you do not, someone will kill you! Or, more likely, a mob will kill you, probably by stoning you or by pulling you apart. Or both!"

"Oh," I replied. "Never before have I fully appreciated the full advantages of being a Jew."

The priest laughed.

"Can you *really* quote all 620 laws?"

"Well, I once got to 610! But my grandmother assured me scornfully that it was *all* of them or it was *none* of them."

I pulled the chain up around my neck, dismissed myself from my judge, and headed straight for the eastern gate. Paul was waiting for me.

"Ah! The chain of approval. Good. Now I will not be obliged to kill you."

"You are a true friend, Paul of Tarsus," I said, answering his tease with a tease. Then I added, in a scolding voice, "You knew how hard that test would be. You could have warned me. *And* you could have told me that without this chain I would be assassinated!"

"Yes, but that would have spoiled everything. Besides, I knew you would be approved. You know your mother's genealogy. That and circumcision are really all they need to know."

"That's all? Then why did that priest pick at me for hours?"

"Oh, they do that sometimes. Otherwise their task would be terribly boring. Now, Timothy, since you are indeed a Jew, I will show you the Holy City."

CHAPTER 3

Jerusalem has a population of about one hundred thousand people but doubles in size during the Passover Festival. Pilgrims come from all over the known world, making Jerusalem a very crowded city indeed.

Many of the people I saw in the streets were incredibly poor. It is beyond my understanding as to how they could afford to come so great a distance. Some came by ship, a few came by horse and wagon, but the largest number came by foot.

In the space of walking fifty feet I saw Syrians, people from Babylon, Yemen, Media, Cyprus, Greece, Egypt, Crete, Asia Minor, and Italy. Some were dark-skinned, others light-skinned, and a few even had blue eyes! They were speaking more languages than can be imagined. Those who came from the West usually spoke either Latin or Greek. Those from the East spoke languages without end.

When Paul and I reached the marketplace, we literally had to push our way in. Before us was an endless line of booths, stands, and tables.

"Anything that is made on this earth you will find here," Paul remarked.

"I believe it," I replied as I stared at the bewildering scene before me.

"Here is bread ground on top of Mt. Ephraim!" cried one merchant. Another shouted, "Here is fish from the Sea of Galilee." Others displayed jewelry that had come from the bowels of the land of Israel. "Gold from the mines of the land of Jacob, a treasure beyond treasure, the finest gold in all the world." On one gold piece I saw written the words: "Made by the goldsmiths of Jerusalem." Phylacteries were on sale everywhere.

I watched as a rich man was being fitted for a beautiful new robe. Next to that booth was a man selling goats. A sandal merchant cried out, "Tell your friends your shoes are from Israel and have trod on holy ground."

There were a few merchants selling parchments with a few words of the Psalms or Isaiah written on them.

Among them all was one appeal: "From the Holy City."

Yet, in all this, the butchers dominated. After all, some two hundred thousand people would eat roasted meat tomorrow evening. They were selling every part of a sheep or goat. "They sell all there is of a sheep except the *baa*," said Paul, quoting an ancient saying.

The price of the sheep was outrageous. The rich paid without blinking an eye. The poor haggled with the butchers for hours.

"Paul, am I fooling myself?" I inquired. "I believe I can make out the Galilean dialect!"

"Not at all. It is an accent thick enough to be noticed even if you cannot speak a word of Aramaic. But the way, the Galileans' dress is probably helping you hear their dialect."

I could not help but ask several older people with that Galilean accent, "Did you see Jesus when he lived in Galilee?" Always they answered the same: "Yes, of course, everyone did."

"Paul, where will all these pilgrims sleep tonight and tomorrow night? I *know* the inns are full."

"By tradition every homeowner in Jerusalem will open his home to guests. There is no charge, but it is understood that a gift will be given for such hospitality. And still there will be more pilgrims than there are homes. Thousands will sleep here in the streets tonight."

"Will we?"

"No, we will be staying in the house of my kinsmen, Andronicus and Junias. They were in Christ before me. They were also the first to tell me of Christ. At the time I was angry with them. Today I am proud of them. They are much loved and respected here, even among the Twelve. It will be an honor for you to meet them. Besides, a bed is softer than stone."

As we pushed farther into the market, I noticed a rising number of Roman soldiers.

"The soldiers have no chain of approval around their necks. Are there always so many soldiers in Jerusalem?"

"With a sword, they need no other approval. But to answer your question, no, I have *never* seen so many soldiers in Jerusalem. *Ever.* The Roman governor will arrive tomorrow. He will reside at Herod's palace, which—as you will see—is more fortress than residence. It is encompassed by great walls and high towers. Things are very tense in Israel. Rome wants no riots when the governor arrives, nor for as long as he is here.

Later that day people began to approach Paul, asking if either of us had yet joined a group to celebrate Passover. (It is customary for people to celebrate the Passover in groups of no less than ten adults. How all these people managed to form these groups is beyond my understanding even to this day.)

Paul had already chosen a group. As for me, Paul advised, "You should not be with me. Find a group to be with. You will enjoy being alone with your own thoughts and emotions during Passover. It will all begin tomorrow. Tomorrow morning we will visit the Temple ground. In late afternoon the Passover sacrifices will begin. In the evening, the Passover meal. You will never forget this day as long as you live."

CHAPTER 4

I never saw so many priests. There must be thousands of them," I said as we entered the streets of Jerusalem just as the sun broke over the city walls.

"And Levites, Timothy. They are all here today. On an ordinary day there is no more than one division of priests serving the Temple and overseeing the sacrifice of animals. But there are twenty-four divisions in all, and today all are present, and all are needed.

"If we lived here, we would be observing the tradition of throwing out all leavened bread from our house. Right now every family is searching their entire home—by the light of an oil lamp—to see if there is any leaven in the house. This ritual will continue into the evening. At that time all leaven in Jerusalem will be burned. It is done all at once, by just one signal. Let us find a place that gives us a clear view of the Mount of Olives, and I will show you.

"See those two oxen pulling a plow? We will wait here until the first ox is unhitched. That is the signal that all eating of leavened bread *stops.* Later, the other ox will be unhitched. That will signal that all leaven is to be burned."

A moment later one of the oxen was unbridled. The crowd

around us cheered. "We will return here later and watch the unhitching of the second ox," said Paul.

Paul and I wandered the city for several hours. At noon the merchants in the city began to close their shops. All selling in the marketplace stopped. The hour for the animal sacrifice was approaching.

At that moment the hills around Jerusalem began turning white. People appeared to come out of nowhere, many carrying sheep as they moved toward Jerusalem.

"There will be three separate sacrifices. Each will last a little less than an hour. The first will begin, oh, about two hours from now," instructed Paul.

"We will be in the first group that brings their sacrifices. It will also have the largest number of people present. But to be in the first group to enter the Temple grounds, we will have to stand for the next two hours packed in among those who arrived at the Temple grounds first."

Sure enough, we were almost crushed by those pushing to get into the courtyard that was before the Temple. When the area was filled, I watched as priests and Levites shut all the gates leading into the Temple grounds.

We waited.

Finally came the blast of trumpets from Levites who were standing on the city walls. A chill came over me as I listened to those silver trumpets resound across the land.

The sacrifice began.

The priests stood before one another in rows. As one, they lifted the gold and silver trays. The first row of priests lifted up gold trays; the second, silver vessels.

Everywhere, praises were being shouted, while all manner of musical instruments accompanied the tumult.

All of us then began saying prayers that we had memorized for this occasion.

The slaughter of sacrifices began.

I was exhausted by the time the ritual was over. Never had I seen such color, pageantry, and beauty.

The gates leading out into the countryside opened, and we moved out quickly. When the courtyard was empty, the priests closed the doors leading to the countryside and opened the doors inside the city, allowing the second group to enter the Temple grounds.

(Paul told me that those going to the third sacrifice were referred to as "the lazy ones.")

As evening approached, the people once more began to move. This time they were returning either to their homes or to a special room set aside for the evening gatherings.

"Look back!" Paul exclaimed. "The Mount of Olives. See!"

The second ox was being unhitched. "From this moment no one will eat leavened bread. All leaven is now being burned."

It seemed everyone we passed in the countryside or in the city was carrying their sacrificed animal or some part of the animal, wrapped in its own skin. These animals, mostly sheep and goats, would soon be roasted. The Night of Redemption had begun.

"Soon you will see the soft glow of fire coming from every home—usually from the courtyard. There the animal sacrifice will be slowly roasted as it turns on the spit," said Paul. "Some will be roasted over a fire of pomegranate wood. Others will be roasting in a clay oven, called the Passover oven.

"Timothy, it is time we parted. You to your group, I to mine. Tomorrow I will spend the day with Peter."

"Peter! You . . . and . . . May I come?"

"I will ask," replied Paul.

"One thing is very important, make no plans for the night of the first day of the week."

"All right. But why?"

"You'll see. Now, may the peace of Israel be with you on this holy night."

I made my way to the home in which I would observe the Passover meal.

I watched breathlessly as the sun set over Jerusalem. The city was completely silent.

The room I stepped into was filled. About half of those present were local Jews; the rest were Greeks who looked a great deal like me.

The Passover meal began with a glass of diluted wine. Next we washed our *right* hands. The roasted lamb was then served along with unleavened bread and bitter herbs. For some reason, I found myself weeping.

At the end of the meal an old man began telling us the ancient story of the first Passover. Once more we sipped diluted wine. One of the youths (who was appointed to do so) asked the question "Why is this night different from all others?" His father then told the story of Israel's deliverance from Egypt. We were all told the meaning of the sacrificial lamb, the unleavened bread, and the bitter herbs as though we had never heard it before. And we all listened just as if it were the first time we had ever heard the story.

Then came the prayer for redemption. Each person prayed for forgiveness for the sins he had committed during the last twelve months. (I longed to declare my Lord who is the *true* Passover. He is the forgiveness of all our sins, and his is a forgiveness that is not just yearly but that stretches into the eternals.)

Once more we drank wine. The ceremony was over.

The oldest of those among us stayed to tell the entire story of the exodus out of Egypt. There were no festivities; it was a night of great sobriety.

I, Timothy, hardly a Jew at all, left the room that night with strange emotions. I felt that I had truly become part of the

Jewish people; yet, at the same time, I knew that my true citizenship rested not on earth, nor was it of any race. My citizenship was in the eternals, and I belonged to a whole new order of things!

I slipped out into the street and made my way to the house of Andronicus and Junias. *Tomorrow will I meet Peter?* I wondered as I fell asleep.

CHAPTER 5

I was shaking all over when we arrived at Peter's home. (Paul, on the other hand, seemed to have his mind on other things.) The man who opened the door was huge. I did not need to ask who he was. It was Peter. He embraced Paul, who virtually disappeared in the embrace. Then he looked down at me.

"Is this the Greek who is passing himself off as a Jew?" asked Peter.

I only managed to mutter, "You have been listening to Silas." (And I was correct, for at that same moment I caught sight of Silas inside Peter's house.)

I had asked myself, *Once they are together, what will Peter and Paul do?* One thing was sure: They were both comfortable with each other. Conflicts of views had long since vanished or were no longer paramount.

Their conversation turned immediately to North Africa, where churches were being born with both Jews and Gentiles present from the beginning. Then they spoke of Corinth. And finally of Rome! When they discussed their burden to share the the gospel *outside* of Israel, Paul spoke of the Gentiles, while Peter referred to his concern for the Jewish people in all foreign lands. Whatever their discussion, Paul managed to bring the topic back to Corinth.

"A large number of the believers in the assembly in Corinth are Jewish. They would be so delighted to see Simon Peter come among them," urged Paul.

"If at all possible," was Peter's assurance.

"I will be leaving tomorrow," explained Paul. "I must not delay my arrival in Antioch. But I do want to thank the assembly in Jerusalem for extending their love and hospitality to me."

"The young man with you, is he a Jew or a Greek? After listening to Silas, I am not sure." Peter was looking straight at me.

"Timothy? He is a Jew in that his mother is Jewish. The rest of the time he is whatever he needs to be at any moment."

Peter laughed. "We would be two blessed men if we could be both Jew and Greek. I have a notion that at this moment you and I are probably the two most disliked believers in Israel."

Paul then shifted the discussion to Cyprus, as Peter was considering going there with Barnabas.

"There is one thing you can do on Cyprus, if you go there as planned," said Paul. "The situation among the churches that were established just after Pentecost is *not* good. The expression of these assemblies is almost like a synagogue. Gentile believers who come to those meetings on Cyprus are confused. They walk into an assembly of Christ that reflects the Jewish culture; consequently they feel like foreigners in their own land. The body of Christ should express Christ through its local culture, not a foreign culture."

Peter agreed. "I will do what I can. When I meet with them, I will do my best to tear down the barrier between these two peoples. Jew and Gentile must find common ground."

There was one other significant point the two discussed that fateful day. It was the way the poorest of the believers in Jerusalem were being treated by the city officials.

"The suffering of the poor believers has to do with taxes, persecution, and inequity," explained Peter.

Peter then expanded on his comment. "Throughout the Western world, Rome taxes everyone *except* the city of Jerusalem. Jews everywhere in the empire are allowed to send their taxes to Jerusalem instead of to Rome. Recently that has changed. The Romans have levied taxes over Israel. The reason they are taxing us is to pay for all the extra soldiers they have been forced to send here! This has caused a great deal of suffering in Israel. The poor simply cannot pay taxes."

Peter dropped his voice. "But there is more than meets the eye. The second largest bank in the world is the Jerusalem Temple. For as long as we Jews can remember, the Temple has always set aside some of its money for the very poor. That is part of the reason why Jews all over the world are so willing to faithfully send their taxes to Jerusalem.

"In the eyes of the Jerusalem priests there are now *two* kinds of poor people: the believers and the unbelievers. Those who run the Temple are ignoring the believers. The poorest among us are not given help by the Jerusalem Temple. This has *never* happened before. The Jerusalem ecclesia is doing all it can, but with the extra taxes *and* the present famine—the crops are terrible—food for the very poor is scarce. So far the ecclesia has managed, but if this drought continues . . . "

Even while Peter was speaking a thought came into Paul's mind: "If the drought continues in Israel, perhaps the Gentile churches to the north could step in and help, thereby meeting the needs of the poor while also strengthening the bond between the Gentile churches and the Jewish churches."

Shortly after that, it came time for Peter and Paul to part.

"Timothy, are you aware that you are to speak to the entire Jerusalem assembly in Solomon's Colonnade?" asked Paul.

"I hear that you can outpreach both Paul and Silas!" laughed Peter. (It was a remark repeated for years to come, which I came to despise the moment anyone quoted it.)

"He outpreaches everyone on earth!" rejoined Paul. "Timothy, try not to do so well in the Colonnade. You do not wish to embarrass Peter and the rest of the Twelve, do you? And remember, *my* Hebrew name is Saul. You need to be reminded that men named Saul are very good at throwing spears—especially at young upstarts!"

"If ever I have told you, Paul, that I felt Christian charity toward you . . . know from this moment on, I lied!" I responded.

With these words the meeting ended.

That night the Jerusalem ecclesia gathered to hear one of their guests. The Jerusalem ecclesia had invited me to speak for the sole reason that they had been fascinated by such a Greek-looking man being so zealous a Jew.

I, in turn, was terrified, especially when I heard that Peter had gone out of his way to be at the gathering. As I stood to speak, I would have gladly changed places with *any* man on earth. That several of the Twelve were present in the gathering did not help.

When I finished, Paul came to my side. "You have learned much from me, young man. You have also told them things I never have thought of. That mother and grandmother of yours raised you well."

"They were enthralled by your young man," said Peter to Silas. "He has a revelation of his Lord. Others of the Twelve made comments to that same end."

(I came to wish I had never spoken in Jerusalem, as some of these remarks reached the Gentile churches and, until this day, I have not lived down the teasing; Titus being the chief instigator.)

"No one ever broke into applause when *I* spoke," said Silas, dryly. "Nor for Peter, either! So the two of us have decided to help Paul purchase a large number of spears to use if ever a thing like this occurs again."

"Agreed," said Paul. "And you are correct—no one has ever broken into applause when *I* spoke either."

The next day Paul and I took our last meal with Silas. It was a memorable occasion. We met in the home of Mary, the sister of Barnabas. It was that same morning that I met John Mark for the first time.

Of all that happened to me that week in Jerusalem, what awed me the most was to see the parchment (which John Mark showed to me) of Barnabas's notes taken in Solomon's Colonnade while sitting at the feet of the Twelve.

Most of the parchment contained stories that the Twelve told about the Lord. When we finished reading everything, I felt that Mark had passed on to me an understanding of the Lord's life while on earth that few had ever heard. All through those wonderful hours I kept urging Mark to rewrite these words into a complete whole.

"You are the second person to urge me to do this," John Mark noted.

"Who was the other?"

"A Gentile brother from Antioch whose name is Titus."

"Titus! The one person I am most desirous to meet when I reach Antioch," I replied.

After that, until the last minute I was in Jerusalem, I kept at Mark. "The Gentiles need a written story of the life of the Lord Jesus. Remember, the Gentile churches are far away from Israel. Things that have happened here, which are commonplace to you, are not easy to understand when living in places such as Galatia and Greece. Write something, please."

Mark finally agreed to discuss the matter with Peter. "I dare not, unless Peter gives full assent."

Early the next morning Silas and Paul bade one another farewell. Between them there were many tears, strong embraces, a prayer, a song, and more tears.

Paul and I then made our way to the north gate. We were met by a number of brothers and sisters from the Jerusalem church who walked with us along the road leading northward to Antioch. As we said our last good-byes, the thought utmost in my mind was: *What hospitality, extended so warmly, to a man who once sought to destroy the Jerusalem ecclesia—and what a warm reception they have given to a half-breed from a Gentile country far away!*

"We really do have a citizenship that breaks the bonds of time, distance, and nationality," I said to Paul as we turned to take one last look at the Holy City.

(As far as what happened to Silas, he remained in Jerusalem for several years. Eventually he made his way to the islands of Greece, most specifically to the isle of Rhodes. It was there, some years later, that Silas was arrested, tried, and sentenced to death.)

After about two weeks of travel, Paul and I reached the southern boundary of Syria. Shortly thereafter we caught sight of the great city of Antioch.

There in Antioch I would encounter the most prevailing assembly I ever saw. It was also there that I would meet Titus, a man destined to be my closest friend. Most of all, though, it was in Antioch that Titus and I would learn from Paul those mysterious plans he was making as he planned his third journey.

As Titus said, "Now *there* is a story worth telling."

CHAPTER 6

"See those men there in the distance? The ones sitting beside the road! Unless I miss my guess, those are *brothers*, waiting to escort us to Antioch."

Paul was right. After a warm greeting all around, one of the men who met us mounted a horse and rode back toward Antioch to inform the brothers and sisters that we would soon be arriving. Then came the great surprise.

"Timothy, tonight you will speak to the church," Paul informed us.

"Tonight? No!" I protested. "You should speak! They want to hear from you, not me!"

"I have been part of the body of Christ in Antioch for eleven years. On the other hand, the believers have never seen you; they have only heard of you. They will desire to hear from you first."

"Well, I have long looked forward to the day when I would see the largest Gentile church in the world, but I did not have any thought of speaking to them—and at the very first meeting I am in!"

As we neared the city, Paul began to reflect on some of his memories. "Barnabas and I learned a great lesson in Antioch.

We are both Jews, but we never for a moment wanted a Jewish influence in the assembly here. God was faithful. The church in Antioch is Gentile to the core. Later, when Barnabas and I went to the land of the Galatians, we found it wise not to stay in any city very long. We are *foreigners.* There was always the possibility that we might introduce our culture, and our ways, to Gentiles. Consequently, we departed from every Gentile church in every Gentile country not long after the birth of the church. This was true of all four of the churches we planted in Galatia . . . including your hometown of Lystra. The only thing of mine that stayed long in Lystra was my blood."

"You are expecting something totally unique in Ephesus? Going to Asia Minor next, are you not?"

"Perhaps," said Paul, still keeping his counsel about why he had chosen to go to that city on his next journey.

"Something different, different from Antioch, different from the Galatian churches, and different from all the churches in Greece?" I prodded.

"Perhaps," Paul replied.

"I *know* that is what you plan. What I want to know is when you are going to tell me what you are hiding?"

"Would telling you . . . oh . . . *perhaps* a week from now satisfy you?" asked Paul.

I jumped into the air and spun around. (The other brothers walking with us had no idea what was going on between the two of us.)

"Soon after we reach Antioch, I will sit down with two young brothers and tell them what it is that I have been planning."

"*One* of them had better be named Timothy," I threatened.

"Oh yes, I think that was the name of one of the brothers I had in mind."

"And the other one? Who is the other one?" I insisted.

"You will find out soon."

At that moment Antioch came into full view.

Just before night we passed into the city through the Daphne Gate. "The streets are lit," I said in full astonishment. "I have never seen such a thing before."

One of the brothers responded, "Nor will you anywhere else in the world. This is the only city on earth that keeps its main avenues lighted by torches all night."

"Not all the streets are lighted?"

"No, only the three major streets leading to the Forum. Nonetheless, it makes our city the safest in the world."

Just as we passed into the city, I saw the amphitheater to my right—and stretched out before me was the grand Street of Colonnades, the most beautiful street in the empire.

"How beautiful. How long is this street?"

"About two miles."

This great avenue ran from the southwest corner of the city to its northeast corner and was thirty feet wide. The surface of the street was marble. There were thirty-two hundred columns on the street. Archways between the columns formed hundreds of porticos. Each portico was thirty-two feet wide, which gave me the sense that we were walking past huge doors on both sides of us. Some of these porticos led to wealthy homes, others to public buildings, and yet others to shops. No other city on earth had anything like this street.

After reaching the end of the Street of Colonnades, we passed out of the city, walking up the slope of a hill. I turned to look back.

"Do not be too impressed," said Paul. "Behind this beautiful street are some of the worst slums in all of the Roman Empire. The people you are about to meet—the Antioch believers—come from *those* places. Although we are going to a villa, most of the people present will be slaves, just as it is in all of the assemblies. We will gather in a garden behind the villa. This is the very same villa to which Barnabas and I came when we returned from Galatia.

"See the lights? That is the garden. After the meeting, there will be a feast, and in the midst of it we will all partake of the Lord's meal."

Songs were wafting across the hills. The assembly had already been together for about an hour. I had no more than stepped into the garden when I was surrounded by dozens of brothers and sisters all trying to embrace me. (I knew that somewhere in that throng was a young man named Titus.) A sense of excitement reigned!

"Finally, you are with us, man from Lystra," someone said.

"That's the brother who stood up to Blastinius," remarked another. My consternation was growing.

"How old is he?" someone asked. I knew exactly what he would answer.

"Older than he looks. Timothy has one of those faces, which, no matter how old he gets, will still look young." I glared at Paul. (Today, as I write this, I am an old man; alas, Paul's words concerning my face turned out to be accurate.)

The crowd encircling me grew until everyone in the garden had formed a huge cluster around Paul and me. We squeezed closely together. They began to sing to me. It was too much. I began crying and couldn't stop.

Finally, Paul made his way to the front of the garden. As he did, there arose a crescendo of praise that then turned into prayer and songs. Paul's words were brief. "You will hear much from me in the days to come. I have much to tell you of Greece. Silas is well and sends greetings from Jerusalem. Luke has kept you informed of all that has happened in these last three years. And, also, our brother Peter sends you his greetings and fond memories of Antioch.

"But tonight belongs to brother Timothy of Lystra. Although he looks Greek, he is—like the ecclesia here in Antioch—part Jewish.

"You will recall that the Jewish believers who arrived in Antioch acted very much like Gentiles. So also does Timothy." (Everyone roared with laughter.) "As to Timothy's age, he is either younger or older than he appears. You must decide which."

Again, there were cheers, crescendos of praise, laughter, and joy interspersed with shouts of exultation.

As rowdy as Corinth, I thought.

"Which one is Titus?" I whispered to someone near me. The answer was drowned out in applause.

I stood to speak. But alas, I only cried.

Finally I began, speaking first of what had happened since my conversion in Lystra. I made sure that every story I told centered around Paul, for I was determined to exalt that brother, his sufferings and sacrifices, and to honor him—just as he had gone out of his way in honoring me.

Antioch was a place where I could speak openly of Blastinius because everyone in the assembly there had met him and observed his conduct, so I held back nothing concerning his efforts to thwart Paul and damage the assemblies.

I recounted all that had happened in northern Greece, including the beating, the imprisonment, and the earthquake. The brothers and sisters wept as they discovered that, once more, Paul had been beaten with rods and banished from a city. He had already suffered so much, as everyone knew.

"Be assured that Paul tried not to be beaten," I said. "He was crying out, 'Civis Romanus sum' as loud as he could."

Then I told them of dear Lydia. Although they had never met her, nor ever knew of her existence before that night, I could see they had fallen in love with her. (They laughed and roared to discover that there existed someone on this earth who could best Paul.)

I then informed them of Blastinius's vow. Although everyone present had heard of this "vow to the death," still many wept. Others moaned. Antioch, I discovered, had a fervent love for Paul.

Then I spoke of Luke's two visits to Asia Minor. (Luke, who was present in the assembly, signaled for me to pass over any further mention of him.)

My goal in reporting to the church in Antioch was not only to give an accurate account of Paul's second journey but also to reveal the deeper implications of these events. I ended by telling them about things that Paul did not realize I knew.

Undoubtedly no one had any idea how frightened and unsure of myself I was that night.

There was one last thing I did. I went out of my way to tell about the money that had come from Philippi to Paul at the time he reached Thessalonica. I described, in no uncertain words, the desperate condition of Paul and Silas at the time the money arrived. I made sure to quote Silas's remark as the two men entered Thessalonica: "I hope the people in the synagogue in Thessalonica like skinny Jews." The garden was as quiet as death when I ended the story.

To Paul's surprise and dismay, I also referred to the crisis Paul went through on the road *to* Thessalonica and stated that none of us would ever really understand the depths of despair that he had passed through as he approached Thessalonica.

(Like everyone else, Paul was weeping uncontrollably as I recounted that ordeal.)

"It is late. Perhaps I can tell you the rest of the story on some future occasion."

There were protests from all over the garden. Nonetheless, I started to sit down, but, instead, questions began coming from all sides of the garden. They laughed with delight as I responded.

Finally, we sang. Oh, did we sing! Half of Antioch must have heard us that night. In Jerusalem, the believers tell of an occasion when prayer was so prevailing that the earth shook. That is the way the meeting in Antioch ended. Praise billowed to heaven; the earth seemed to quake under our feet.

Once again I attempted to sit down, but once again the entire gathering moved forward and enclosed Paul and me. In one final accolade, we lifted our hearts and voices to the Lord in thanksgiving.

At this point I noticed that someone was pushing his way toward me, and I instinctively knew who it was. I found myself pushing toward him as well. Everyone began to cheer. As we neared one another, he yelled, "I am Titus!"

"I know!" I shouted back. "And I am Timothy."

We threw our arms around one another and hugged each other with all our strength, all the time mingling prayers, praise, and tears, laughing and crying at the same time. I, Timothy, was bound to that brother that night and have remained so to this very hour. The meeting began all over again as others joined in our shouts and tears. It was almost dawn before everyone left the garden.

Arm in arm, Titus and I walked through the streets and finally came to the house where I would be staying. (I lodged in the same place where Paul always lived when in Antioch—the home of Simon called Niger.)

As the sun broke over the horizon, Titus and I fell on our faces before God and prayed our hearts out, offering prayers not even fools would dare. We asked that Jesus Christ might be known throughout the entire Gentile world and that the bride of Christ would one day walk across the face of the entire earth. At last, utterly exhausted, we both fell asleep there on the floor.

A few hours later Paul came in, saw us asleep, and smiled knowingly, for he had known such hours in the early years after his own conversion. We later learned that the sight of two young men, who had fallen asleep on their faces while in the presence of God, had meant a great deal to him.

The next day marked the beginning of the greatest week of my life—a statement to which Titus would fully agree.

CHAPTER 7

Two sleepy-eyed young men did not awake until almost noon the next day.

That morning Titus introduced me to the family with whom I would be staying. You have heard of them. Simon, called Niger, is the man who carried the Lord's cross. He had been soundly converted on the day of Pentecost and years later moved to Syria in order to be part of the gathering in Antioch. Simon was also one of the five men present when the Holy Spirit separated Paul and Barnabas to take the gospel to the Gentiles.

Simon has two sons, Rufus and Alexander, both well known to this day as faithful followers of Christ. (Rufus eventually moved to Rome.)

Simon's wife, who cooked our breakfast that morning, was one of the kindest, most thoughtful souls I had ever known. Paul, when in Antioch, lived in Simon's home, and it was Simon's wife who looked after Paul's every need.

We spent the entire afternoon listening to Rufus and Alexander tell the story of their lives and that of their father and mother.

Late that afternoon Simon arrived. I begged him to tell me

the details of that awful day as he carried the Lord's cross to Golgotha.

Although Titus had heard the story before, there was something different that day in Simon's recollection. He knew, better than we, that he was speaking to two future workers in the Lord's kingdom. He wanted us to know the story, *all* of it.

At first we were enthralled. Then we cried. So did Simon. Rufus and Alexander joined in the tears, and Titus and I lost complete control of ourselves. Simon held us both in his huge arms, the very arms that once cradled the cross! Simon's wife and their two sons joined in the embrace. We became one great cataract of tears. It ended with Simon, in that deep, strong voice praying for us, telling, not asking—the Lord to send these two men to the ends of the earth with the message that Jesus is the Christ.

In the days that followed, I went everywhere asking questions. I made Titus tell in minute detail about his trip to Jerusalem with Paul and Barnabas. About Peter, the Twelve, and James, the Lord's brother. And like everyone else who heard Titus tell the story of the Pharisees who tried to spy out his freedom, I convulsed with laughter as he told of running out in the Jerusalem streets naked while yelling at the Pharisees, "I have exactly as much skin as Abraham did on the day God reckoned Abraham as righteous!"

Titus, in turn, wanted to hear every detail of Paul's entry into Lystra on his first journey and a day-by-day account of Paul's second journey to Greece.

We both shared our experiences of meeting Blastinius Drachrachma (the Pharisee who insisted that all Christians obey the laws of Moses and be circumcised and was set on Paul's destruction).

I told Titus about all four of the churches in Galatia: how each was *unique* and how each existed for years without leaders or outside help. I told him of Lydia and gave him a detailed account of the beating and imprisonment of Silas and Paul.

Titus wept as I shared with him the desperate hours Paul spent on the road to Thessalonica . . . and the gift that came from Philippi.

We talked on and on about the Lord's work, about Blastinius's every effort to destroy Paul, and of the growing hatred toward Paul that was coming forth from Israel . . . most of which was stirred up by Blastinius.

Throughout our lives Titus and I were so much of one mind. When I called him *brother*, it was far more than a word, for we were closer than brothers.

I also told Titus all I knew about Paul's mysterious plans—which was very little. (I did not tell him that the name of the city Paul intended to visit was Ephesus. I wanted that to be a surprise.) I also told Titus that Paul had promised to tell me his "mystery" within a week.

During the following days of anxious waiting, I spent every moment absorbing all I could of the history of the assembly in Antioch: its beginning, its growth, the crisis through which it had passed, and how the assembly managed all those years without *ever* having elders.

I asked to see the room where the Holy Spirit had set apart Paul and Barnabas.

I fear I drove many to distraction asking about the things Barnabas and Paul had spoken on during the early years of the church in Antioch. I even went down to the port of Seleucia, from which Paul and Barnabas first set sail in order to reach Cyprus. I went to a gathering of brothers and watched how—together—they came to their decisions. (I even was invited to a meeting of my sisters in Christ, there to see again that women are always wiser in their ways than we brothers ever are.)

I wanted to see the hall where Paul confronted Peter but

was met with this reply: "Brother Timothy, we are trying to forget that day."

One of the great privileges I had was to visit the assemblies in some of the villages and towns near Antioch. All these gatherings had been raised up by brothers and sisters in the Antioch church. (They were the ones who also planted a string of churches all up the northern coast of Syria.)

Titus told me that Paul was both amazed and pleased at hearing of all my "annoying" questions. But I was not the only one asking questions. Someone else was just as busy asking *me* questions: Titus's uncle, Luke!

Luke sat down with me, asking every detail of what had happened when Paul and Barnabas came to Galatia. He insisted that I tell the story, in detail, about Greece, Philippi, Berea, and especially Thessalonica!

For long hours he asked me about the city of Corinth. "Which roads did you take to get to the port? What port did Paul leave from? What kind of ship was it? How long did the voyage take?" Sometimes I felt Luke knew more about Paul's second journey than I did.

(Today, I, Timothy, am so grateful that Luke did all this. I had no idea he would later write all these events down in a book, but how glad the Gentiles are that he did. Otherwise we would know neither our own story nor the Jerusalem story.)

As the week came to an end, Titus and I became anxious to hear from Paul. True to his word, Paul asked the two of us to come into his room. What we heard we shall never forget.

CHAPTER 8

"Would you two brothers meet me this evening?" were words Titus and I had waited to hear ever since my arrival in Antioch.

That evening we came into Paul's room and sat down on the floor. Paul looked first at Titus, then at me.

"Sometime ago I wrote a letter to all the churches in Galatia and Greece. I have waited until now to speak to you because I have been waiting for their response. More recently I have also sought out the wisdom of some of the brothers and sisters here in Antioch. I have now heard their response. It is time I tell you of my plans."

Paul's next words amazed us.

"You have asked about my plans—here they are: I desire to do something that my Lord did when he was on earth. For three years he trained *twelve* men. He walked with them, lived with them—he *trained* them. Then . . . after that . . . he sent them out to the Jews. Those twelve men were better prepared for their task than any other men in history. Trained by the Lord Jesus Christ, they went out to the Hebrews. In Israel they proclaimed Christ and planted the church."

Paul searched the eyes of the two men sitting before him. "That *same* Lord has sent *me* to the Gentiles. Unfortunately, our Lord is not physically present to train a group of Gentile men to take Christ and the church to the heathen nations. It is not possible for a group of young Gentiles to be sent out by Christ. The Lord will not train Gentile workers. But *someone* must!

"I am told there are about one or two million Jews in Israel. Jesus sent out twelve men to only one million people. On the other hand, Priscilla tells me that the population of the Roman Empire alone is 75 *million!* Seventy-five million people—yet only Barnabas, Silas, and I have been *sent* to all these heathen. Not very proportionate, is it? Twelve men to one million; *three* men to 75 million. And all three of us are *Jews!*

"*Not a single Gentile worker. Not one Gentile who plants churches. This must change!* There must be Gentile workers, men to carry on the Lord's work when we three are gone." Paul then looked at me and added, "Of course, there is one young man who can go to either the Jews or the Gentiles."

"Timothy, you're blushing," said Titus.

"He often does," replied Paul.

"I have reached that point in my life when it is time for me to train Gentile men who have been called of God. Someone must carry on the work after I am gone. There are *many* men to take the place of the Twelve, but as of now, there are *none* to take my place."

Neither of us was breathing.

"Who will I train? Do you know of such men? Even if I did not know their names, I *know* what kind of men I would train. There are qualifications they *must* meet."

Titus groaned.

"I will train men who have lived in the life of the ecclesia, *no one else.* If they have not lived in the ecclesia, I will not train them. Second, I will train men who profess to be called of God."

Paul's next words were sad. "There are so very, very few.

Few Gentile churches, few believers, and almost no men called of God."

"I have been called," snapped Titus.

"So have I," I growled.

"Shhh!" said Paul, still speaking in not much more than a whisper.

"I have watched a dozen young Gentile men who thought they had been called. Most of them were dreamers . . . and still are."

Paul sighed. "My point is this. I am looking for *evidence* of that call. I look around and see little evidence of that call in the lives of most. How many burn for Jesus Christ? Who . . . anywhere . . . burns for the church? Who can, and *does*, suffer the Cross? My choices are few, indeed.

"One last thing I demand of such men—the most important of all! Any man I train must first have the blessing of the church in which he grew up. It doesn't matter what a man *thinks* he is; the church *knows* him better than he will ever know himself. Anyone I train must receive the full approval of the church with which he assembles."

Paul stopped abruptly.

"Jesus lived with twelve men for three years. Now I tell you this. I, Paul, am going to gather together a group of men—a number *smaller* than *twelve*—and I shall live with them for three or four years."

"Where?" blurted Titus.

Paul did not answer.

"I want to say again, no one will be trained by me unless he was first nothing more than a simple brother in the church. And once those men are trained, I pray that by God's mercy they will always be *itinerant*. Traveling. *Never* settling down with one church. To stay in one church would be disastrous to that church. Those men must *never* do this."

"*How* will you train them?" I asked.

"They will walk with me wherever I go. They will learn by watching and listening. Then, finally, by *doing*. They will learn in the reality of ordinary church life. I will not train men the way the Jews and Greeks train—not by theory and not by lectures. I am *not* Gamaliel, and I am *not* Aristotle."

Titus asked his question again: "*Where* will it be?"

"It will be Ephesus."

I grabbed Titus and hugged him, though I know he had only the vaguest idea as to the location of Ephesus.

"And how many will be there?" asked a breathless Titus.

"Six."

"That is half the number Jesus trained," replied Titus, with obvious disappointment.

Paul ignored the comment.

"I have written to every one of the churches that have come from my hand, asking them, 'Is there *unquestionably* such a young man among you?'

"Of course, I did not write a letter to Antioch."

"You did not ask Antioch?" exploded Titus.

"That is not what I said. We are, after all, *in* Antioch. Do I need to write a letter here? In Antioch I had only to ask. This afternoon I met with some of the brothers and sisters . . . to see if they concur or disapprove of my choice."

Titus slapped both hands on top of his head, then sank, head first, to the floor. "Oh no. And to think of all the mistakes I've made here. I am doomed."

Again Paul ignored Titus but not quite as successfully as before. (I noted a stifled smile.)

"When I wrote the churches, I asked if they could see anyone among them called of God. Someone who has lived in the church. Someone who has the church's confidence. Brothers, the churches were very honest with me. Some have no such person among them. No man will be trained unless his home church places its blessing on that man. You must know that a few men were *very, very* offended because they were not chosen. This, in itself, is evidence that they are not men I wish to train."

Titus was still headfirst on the floor, moaning.

Paul, still ignoring him, continued, "When I wrote to one particular church, I told them that a brother who once lived among them would probably not be back ever again, except to visit."

"That's me! That's Lystra! I'm going to Ephesus!" I cried.

"But Antioch? Paul, what did the Antioch believers say to you?" asked Titus, finally.

"They are all in agreement."

"Paul of Tarsus! Do not make me suffer anymore. Who did Antioch select?" demanded Titus.

Paul smiled. "Luke's nephew."

There was an instant of silence as we both tried to figure out who was the nephew of Luke.

Titus jumped to his feet. "That's *me.* I'm Luke's nephew!" He reached down, pulled me to my feet, and hugged me. He proceeded to whirl me around the room and then grabbed Paul, shouting and laughing as he did.

"I assume, brother Titus, this means you are willing to go to Ephesus with me."

"Yes! Yes!"

By now Titus and I were shaking one another with all our might. When we had regained enough of our senses, we asked a most obvious question: "Who are the other four? What churches have men to send?"

"The church in Derbe has approved . . . "

"It's Gaius, I know it is!" I exclaimed. Paul did not bother to finish his sentence.

"Where else? *Who* else?" Titus asked.

"Thessalonica."

Once more I blurted out, "It's Aristarchus and Secundus. It has to be!"

"Why do I bother answering your questions? *You*, it seems, have already made my selections for me."

"Is it? Am I right? It's got to be Aristarchus and Secundus!"

Paul grabbed me and began shaking me. "Yes! Yes! Yes, it is Secundus and Aristarchus." We hugged Paul again, lifting him off the ground as we did.

"But that's just five," said Titus. "Who else?"

"Sopater of Berea."

"Hallelujah!" I cried, at the top of my lungs. "This is sheer bliss!"

A lifetime has passed since that unforgettable evening. I, Timothy, look back and realize what an astounding thing Paul did in that hour. He took upon himself the ways of Jesus Christ as he lived out those ways in Galilee. That day Paul had spoken his own "come follow me." He chose six men to train.

I have been at Paul's side as he planted assemblies in the heathen world, but that day I saw Paul do something he had never done before. He boldly issued a call to called men. Later, he *sent* those men.

And six men heard. And six men followed!

One of the highest honors of my life was that I, along with Titus, was in that room that day when Paul's fondest dream first came to light.

Jesus Christ was not on this earth to train us, but Jesus Christ had left church planters on this earth. It was for them to train men. The planters of churches, and they alone, are to train men for the work. *That* is the heritage Paul passed on to us that evening.

Despite the fact that the churches from which we came knew us so well (*too* well), they sent their full approval. All six of the men who went to Ephesus *were* called. All six came as ordinary brothers from churches. All six were trained. All six were later *sent.* All six remained faithful.

As surely as the Twelve had followed Christ, had lived together with him, had been called and then *sent* by him . . . so we six were called by the Holy Spirit, were trained together by a church planter, and were finally *sent out* by the churches *and* the Holy Spirit. Since that hour, all six men have planted churches in the Gentile world. We six have done in heathendom what the Twelve did in Israel.

Paul's plan was the greatest single stroke of genius to come forth from his ministry. To gather six men from five churches and take them to Ephesus was surely the way of God for all future workers. We came from Syria, Galatia, northern Greece, and southern Greece. We came from four provinces and three cultures. Among the six of us, a total of four languages was spoken, as well as numerous local dialects.

Each of us had come from different assemblies. Each assembly had a different background, expression, and history. Each church and, therefore, each brother had a different story to tell to the others of us. Every one of us could say, "Paul came into my city and preached the gospel, and the church was born. *And I was there from the very beginning.*"

I, Timothy, was the only one who previously knew all of the other five men. Not only could each of us say, "I was there from the beginning," but later—after three years in Ephesus—we could all add, "I was there from the beginning, twice!"

It was later, after Paul had begun to train us, that Titus and I realized Paul would train us by means not known on earth at that time. Paul was a revolutionary, and the way he trained was revolutionary. We did not learn by rote. We did not sit at the feet of a man and write down what he said, memorize it, and then regurgitate it. Twenty-four hours a day, seven days a week, we lived with church problems, pressures, misunderstandings, and persecution. Together we experienced *reality*.

In the midst of all this joy, at this same moment things were happening in the church in Corinth that would eventually throw that church into a grave crisis.

CHAPTER 9

His name was Apollos.

Even until this day it is difficult to fully understand both the contribution and the damage caused by Apollos in the church in Corinth.

Here is the story.

One day a man arrived at the Jewish synagogue in Ephesus. Apollos was Jewish, but his training and his occupation were Gentile. His father and mother were Jews from Alexandria, Egypt. Apollos knew the Scripture and had a heart to know God. In his pursuit of God he had heard of John the Baptist and John's prediction of a coming Messiah. Apollos had accepted John's message but had not yet heard of Jesus nor of his death and resurrection.

In the Ephesian synagogue, Apollos spoke fervently and boldly about the coming Messiah. Hearing him, one might think he had actually heard of Jesus and believed that Jesus was the Messiah. Yet the fact was, Apollos knew only the message John the Baptist had spoken concerning the Christ.

By occupation, Apollos was a traveling philosopher and orator in the tradition of the *Sophisticates.* (He received pay for speaking at banquets, weddings, funerals, and other special occasions.)

Apollos was the greatest orator any of us ever heard. (This was both Apollos's greatest strength and his greatest weakness.)

It was in the synagogue in Ephesus that Priscilla and Aquila first heard Apollos.

There, as in all other places where he spoke, Apollos could make his audience laugh uproariously one minute and bring them to tears the next.

(Priscilla observed, "Growing up in Rome, I had heard great Greek and Roman orators ever since I was a child, but I had never heard anyone who even came close to having the skills of this man.")

After the synagogue ritual concluded, one of the God-fearers asked Apollos to come visit the home of a friend who was gravely ill. As you know, it is the custom among heathen to bring a philosopher to the bedside of one who is dying, in order to speak words of consolation. (Such was one of the ways Apollos earned his living.)

The next Sabbath Apollos spoke again, outdoing even his first oration. It became evident to Priscilla and Aquila, however, that Apollos had never heard the account of the Lord Jesus Christ!

Priscilla asked Apollos to come to their home for the noon meal. There Priscilla presented the gospel of Jesus Christ to Apollos. He responded without hesitation. She then urged Apollos to go immediately to a city where there was an assembly of believers. She recommended Corinth. In doing so, Priscilla expected Apollos to settle there, seek employment, and become a brother—among brothers—in the assembly there.

Unfortunately, Apollos went on with his ministry, never knowing church life.

Could Apollos have endured the exposure of being in the church? We will never know. From the day of his conversion until the day he died in Spain, Apollos never became part of the daily experience of the body of Christ. He lived and died a traveler.

(When Apollos was asked why he never became a brother in the church, his answer was always the same: "The day is dark, the hour is late. Jesus will be returning any day now. The time is too short to do anything but preach!")

Apollos's skill was greater than his revelation, his gifts far greater than his transformation. Not only did he never live within the church; he had no revelation of the centrality of the church. He rarely referred to the Cross as it pertains to the life of the believer. Nor did Apollos know much of the Cross in his own life. The word *loss* was not in the vocabulary of his ministry.

It was the wisdom of Priscilla that caused her to say to this brilliant orator, so new in Christ, "You should join yourself to one of the assemblies. Become a brother in that assembly. Perhaps, at some future date, you will be ready to enter into the Lord's work on the earth."

Corinth was perfect for Apollos, a man who was Greek both in culture and in thought. A few days later he left Ephesus and set sail for Greece. His relationship to Corinth later proved to be disastrous for the assembly there.

Apollos arrived in Corinth at the same time that Paul was leaving Antioch to go to Ephesus. Little could we imagine that with the arrival of Apollos in southern Greece, the foregleams of a major crisis were beginning in the church in Corinth.

CHAPTER 10

Apollos arrived in Corinth with a letter from Priscilla and Aquila telling of his background and conversion. The ecclesia received him warmly, especially because the letter was from the much beloved Aquila and Priscilla. In the next meeting, as customary, Apollos shared his testimony of Christ. The Corinthians were awed by Apollos's speaking ability.

Men who speak well are usually perceived as also being spiritual. Unfortunately, the two do not always go together. Apollos was given lodging with one of the unmarried brothers, of course, and was expected to become a brother among brothers. A few days later Apollos asked to speak again in the meetings.

Apollos had a deep, resonating, baritone voice; he was a master at holding his audience as well as a master of the Scriptures. Once again the brothers and sisters were awestruck. It was soon whispered that one greater than Paul had come to us! (And that statement was true if you counted *only* Apollos's speaking skills and nothing more.)

Soon Apollos spoke in virtually all the meetings. Eventually the time of singing grew shorter. There were only a few songs, a few prayers, virtually no sharing, and *then* Apollos. The functioning of the body of Christ lessened.

As was the nature of Apollos, he announced that he would be traveling to other places in Greece and Macedonia to preach the gospel. He then did something that was unprecedented among the Gentile ecclesia: He asked the Corinthian ecclesia to pay him to travel to these places in order to preach. The dear Corinthians gave an enthusiastic yes.

Apollos visited Berea, then Thessalonica. The holy ones in Philippi, as they do in all the Gentile gatherings, received their guest warmly. After spending some time there, he departed for Alexandria.

Later, Apollos returned to the church in Corinth. It was his presence there that later created a crisis that almost destroyed the church—and broke the heart of Paul of Tarsus. (As Paul once wrote: "A man ought to be careful how he builds on *another* man's foundation.") Apollos had not been too careful how he built on the foundation Paul had laid in Corinth.

In the meantime, we—Paul, Titus, and I—were simply going about getting ready for our journey to Ephesus. It would still be a few years before Paul found himself faced with the problems created by Apollos's carelessness in Corinth, not to mention the crisis created by Blastinius and by the Daggermen. All three came at once.

Just before we left Antioch, we received several wonderful letters from four wonderful young men.

CHAPTER 11

The first letter came from Derbe: Gaius assured us that he would be awaiting our arrival. (Paul planned to pass through Galatia on our way to Ephesus.)

Shortly thereafter came a letter from Greece: Sopater of Berea would travel to Asia Minor and await our arrival in Troas!

Then came a letter from Thessalonica: Secundus and Aristarchus would join with Sopater as he passed through Thessalonica. The three of them would also wait for our arrival in Troas.

Each brother related in his letter how his assembly had laid aside enough money to cover his travel expenses to Ephesus and how the gathering planned to give him a royal send-off.

Paul's route would take us along the northern coastline of Syria and then into Galatia. From there we would travel north and west to Asia Minor, going first to Troas. From there six men and Paul would enter Ephesus together.

Twenty-four years had passed since Pentecost. The church in Antioch was now fourteen years old.

We were only hours from departing when a letter arrived from Silas in Jerusalem. His letter was very disturbing. Tension in Israel was growing by the day. The Daggermen had now become a very effective force in Israel, not to mention a source of sheer terror. This league of assassins had taken a vow to kill anyone who diluted the traditions of Moses, and they were determined to assassinate any Jews who derived their wealth from being in league with Rome. The Daggermen had been debating whether or not Paul should be one of those assassinated. But Silas's most telling words were these: "Paul, you should know that you have become the center of controversy here in Jerusalem."

I watched Paul as he read the letter. I saw no indication of fear. He had already died to the abuses of local governments, had learned patience with the churches, and was in the process of seeing his flesh die to the ever-present threat of Blastinius. Paul also knew he still lived outside the full approval of the Jewish believers as a whole. In all of this he never allowed a root of bitterness to grow up in him. He had learned to lose—to lose and lose again—as few men ever had. In hearing of the assassins' debate, he was concerned for the welfare of the Gentile churches. What would happen to these churches in the event of his death?

Silas's letter sealed Paul's determination to go to Ephesus and train men to take his place. Just before we left Antioch, he called Titus, Luke, and me together for a talk. "My life may be cut short. Eight years ago Barnabas and I set out from here and went to Cyprus. After leaving Cyprus we traveled to where the gospel had never before been preached.

"Now, because of the faithfulness of the church in Antioch in standing with us, the gospel has been taken not only to Galatia but also up the coast of Syria and into Cilicia. Because of this, there is now less than a seventy-mile gap between the *last* church located in Syria and the *first* church located in Galatia. God willing, I will see the ecclesia born in Ephesus, which is only a three-day journey by ship to northern Greece. Brothers, in case my life is cut short, you must one day plant the church of Jesus Christ on the west side of Greece, in Illyricum and in Dalmatia. I need not tell you why." Paul's eyes twinkled. "But I will! From western Greece and Illyricum you are a short distance across the Adriatic Sea from Italy. From those shores . . . Rome!

"If I die, you Gentiles *must* take the gospel to Rome."

Luke interrupted, "If Claudius becomes a god, and if the Daggermen do not get to you, then *you* will go to Rome."

"This is my hope, but I understand Claudius is in very good health." Paul's next words were sweeping in their declaration. "It is my passionate hope that a day will come when a man can leave Jerusalem, walk through Syria and Cilicia, turn west and go into Galatia, and from there, north and west into the very heart of Asia Minor—never being more than three- or four-days' journey from a city, town, or village where there is a gathering of the ecclesia of Jesus Christ. *This* is my hope—my dream."

(Paul did not live to see *why* God had laid this on his heart. The day came, after Jerusalem was destroyed, when thousands of believers fled Israel. Everywhere they went, if they went north, there was a Gentile church along the way waiting to protect them and help them on their way or receive them into their midst.)

Paul continued, "A day must come when believers can leave Rome, cross over to Illyricum, then go down to Greece, sail from Greece straight to Ephesus, turn south, and go all the way to Jerusalem without being far from the ecclesia of Jesus Christ. Brothers, should I die, planting these churches will be *your* task."

"The thought of how . . . to establish the ecclesia in Rome . . . staggers me," said Luke. "I hope you live long enough to be the one who goes there. This is a task far beyond the rest of us."

Paul's answer was one of confidence: "Old Claudius is not the first person to order us Hebrews out of Rome. The emperor Tiberius threw us out some ten years before the Lord Jesus began his ministry. Tiberius changed his mind. It seems we Jews were the only people honest enough to keep business going in Rome. We can thank Moses and his 620 laws for our honesty. Perhaps Claudius will do what Tiberius did and wake up to this same fact."

What Paul said to us that day was kept hidden in our hearts for years to come. Paul's only other comment was about Silas's letter: "I am concerned for the safety of Simon Peter. The Daggermen will one day put him on their list. As long as Peter remains in Israel, he is in great danger."

Paul then added a word that had a ring of the prophetic. "I fear there will be war in Israel. When it comes, there will be hundreds of thousands of Jews fleeing. Some will go to Egypt. If so, I hope there will be Gentile believers there to receive them. Jewish believers who flee northward *will be* warmly received by the Gentile churches.

"Now," he said with finality, "you two young men go and pack. There are four other young men waiting to meet us along the way . . . to Ephesus!"

The church in Antioch was fourteen years old. It was summer. Claudius was emperor. Some twenty-four years had passed since the resurrection of Jesus Christ. And Gentile workers were about to be trained.

CHAPTER 12

The next morning about five hundred brothers and sisters marched with us through the Daphne Gate, singing along the way. They continued with us for an hour. They turned back to Antioch only after the sun broke over the horizon.

Titus had never been north. Neither of us had ever visited the churches in northern Syria or Cilicia.

You might say our training began that day.

As we moved along the coast, we rarely walked more than three days without coming to a town or village where we were hosted by a church. There, in every assembly, we learned something new about the church of Jesus Christ—how she was planted, how she grew.

"I did not realize how many new churches had been born," noted Titus. "The brothers in Antioch have carried the gospel and the church up and down the coast."

Eight years earlier there had been no churches along the coastline. Now, here we were spending at least two or three nights in these churches all along our route. The entire journey up the coast was pure joy.

I must confess, though, that the nicest part of the journey was that neither Titus nor I had to carry bags of food from one city to another.

(Years later, arriving in Rome after a desperate sea journey, Paul commented, "Not quite as easy a trip as the one we made together to Ephesus!")

We were less than a hundred miles from my hometown of Lystra when we turned northwestward. Our first stop in Galatia was Derbe. Gaius was waiting to join us.

Titus was beside himself to finally visit a church located in Galatia. He was acting the way I did when I first came to visit Jerusalem and Antioch.

Meeting with the Derbe assembly was a great moment for all of us. Brothers and sisters from the other three Galatian churches (Pisidia, Iconium, and Lystra) had come to Derbe to see us. (Eunice, my mother, was there, embarrassing me as mothers do.)

I need not tell you that Gaius was as excited as Titus and I. Our first night in Derbe the three of us stayed up all night talking. It did not take long to understand why Paul—and the church in Derbe—had chosen Gaius. He was a pioneer and evangelist at heart, the wildest of us all, and ready to go anywhere at any time.

Paul spent several days with the brothers and sisters from the other three Galatian churches. After that, we departed Derbe and made our way over to those churches. And in every one of these cities we three young men learned new things about the Lord's work on earth.

One thing stood out to me as we visited the Galatian believers. There were now brothers in every one of the churches who ministered the Word, even Christ. And in all four churches there were brothers and sisters who could encourage, exhort, and admonish the ecclesia. Nor did my fellow Galatians hesitate to open their mouths in the meetings. The churches in Galatia were growing up in Christ and doing so with a past history of so little outside help. To me it was a miracle. Although the church in Antioch had been *mostly* Gentile, the churches in Galatia were *truly* Gentile. Nor were they like any church in Syria or Cilicia, which we had just visited.

Paul said it best: "The churches have grown in number! And even in a bit of wisdom."

It was true. In the first four or five years there had been little growth in the Gentile churches. But now the brothers (especially those who were there from the beginning) had matured enough to take care of new ones coming into the assembly. Then, following that, ingathering had begun.

Gaius, ever the one to ask the hard questions, said to Paul, "You have planted only one church in each province in Galatia. As soon as you plant just one church in each province, you then state that the province has been evangelized. Explain."

"One church in each province is enough," replied Paul. "The brothers and sisters in the assembly will carry the gospel to the other towns in their province. It is the *church* that will plant churches."

Paul stared at Gaius for a long moment, then added, "Gaius, do you understand what I just said?"

"Yes, I understand. The four churches in Galatia are going to be very busy."

Paul smiled and continued, "The first church to be raised up in any province needs much time. Even in Israel—that is, in Jerusalem—this was true. For the first seven years after the Lord's ascension there was only one church on this earth.

"The Antioch church came out of Jerusalem. The Gentile churches in Galatia came into being as a result of Antioch. Antioch was the bridge. All the Gentile churches have come forth from Antioch. But it took time for all these things to blossom. Do not expect great numbers to come out of a new work. Foundations take time! That is because the work of the Cross and the transformation of souls take time."

This was only Paul's third visit to Galatia—three visits in eight years. In each assembly he spent a day or two with all of the brothers. Then, on another occasion he spent another day or two with the women. Finally he spoke to the entire assembly for several days. After that, we left.

I, Timothy, will not seek to explain the depth of the love the four Galatian churches had for Paul, nor the churches' love for one another.

After just one month in Galatia, including the time spent walking from one province to another, we turned our faces toward Asia Minor. For the first few days we were accompanied by some of the Galatian believers. But eventually they turned back, and we were left alone.

As we moved along the road, we began to notice the road markers that told us how many miles it was to Ephesus. Each marker told us we were one mile closer to "the beautiful city."

Not far away, as we moved north, there were three Greeks moving southward to meet us. And when we met, what a day!

CHAPTER 13

When we arrived in Troas, our three brothers from northern Greece were waiting for us.

I, Timothy, cannot tell you what that day was like. Seven of us together! There was a great deal of hugging and shouting and praising the Lord. By nightfall, Paul retired to his room. We six talked, laughed, told stories, and laughed again throughout the night and into the next day.

Gaius and Titus listened intently as our Greek brothers told the story of what had taken place from the first day Paul entered Philippi.

We fell asleep just before noon.

Paul woke us up *far* too soon. He insisted that we leave *immediately* for Ephesus. There were groans from all of us until he admitted that he had already arranged for us to spend another night at the inn. Paul obviously knew what a group of young single brothers was like.

That afternoon and on into the evening the seven of us talked yet again. Paul spent hours sharing with us much that was on his heart. One of the things he shared with the brothers from Greece was his desire to see a church planted in Illyricum.

"It is just north of Greece, and it is only a short distance across the Adriatic Sea from Italy. As I have already told Titus and Timothy, if I die before this is done, I hold you three Greeks responsible for planting a church in Illyricum."

Paul then made a statement as blunt as a man could make. "Jesus Christ once warned that Jerusalem would be surrounded and that those in Israel should flee. Peter and I are very concerned that the gospel, and the ecclesia, be planted in North Africa in preparation for that day. For those Hebrews who flee northward, it is my passion that as the Jewish believers enter Gentile countries, they be received by *Gentile* churches, not Jewish churches.

"In that day it must not be as it is in Cyprus—a Gentile land, but with churches that are Jewish in expression. A Gentile there must become part of a foreign culture if he is to be in the Lord's assembly. If Jews go into the *Gentile* world, they must expect the churches to be Gentile in nature. On the other hand, if Gentiles go to Israel, they must become part of the Jewish way of church life."

Paul grew very somber. "I only pray to God that the unity between the Jewish and Gentile churches holds. You are Gentiles. Be gentle and understanding if the Jews flee into your world. Today they do not ask you to be circumcised into a Jewish world. Do not ask them to be circumcised into yours."

Paul then went on to tell us some of the things he expected of us and what he planned to do with us and *to* us!

There was much prayer that evening.

The next morning six young men, all between the ages of twenty-five and thirty, set out for Ephesus. We were as excited as young men can be, hugging one another, singing and praising the Lord, shouting ridiculous prayers to God. Despite our youthful foolishness, Paul had a glow on his face, reflecting his own private joy about this hour.

Sometimes we walked six abreast. Having grown a little

weary of our youthful exuberance and chatter, Paul began to walk a good distance in front of us. I have made many journeys in my life, but those hours were perhaps the most memorable traveling days I can recall. We were about to come into a new city to live with Paul for three years!

A short distance from Ephesus we stopped, grabbed Paul, and pulled him into the middle of a circle. We pressed as close to one another as we possibly could and began to sing, pray, and weep. So began our last mile toward Ephesus.

Just a few minutes later we caught sight of *Ephesus, the beautiful!* Upon that sighting, we stopped, knelt in the middle of the road, and prayed. Oh, how we prayed! And none prayed more fervently than Paul.

For several days the thought uppermost in our minds was *How will Paul begin?*

All six of us knew the importance of *being there from the beginning.* We six were all there, in our respective churches—from the beginning. We wanted to see Paul do a new "from the beginning."

How long would it take to begin? Who would be the first converts? How would those first believers come to Christ? Would Paul begin in the synagogue or the marketplace? If in the synagogue, what would be the results? How long would it be from the moment we entered that city until that first gathering of the Lord's assembly? How *difficult* would it be to begin? As difficult as Lystra, Iconium, or Thessalonica? In a word: Just how *does* this Paul start a church in untouched places?

We got our answer! You might even say the ecclesia in Ephesus was born *before* we reached Ephesus.

We had walked only a few feet beyond the place where we had stopped to pray when we saw twelve men gathered in a small cluster not far off the road. They were praying fervently.

This, in itself, was hard to believe. Greeks and Romans do not do such a thing.

Paul stepped off the road and walked toward them—no more than thirty feet. He stopped and listened. He then interrupted. "I am Paul. A Jew. Are you men of my persuasion?"

"No, we are not Jews," was the response. "We are Greeks. We are what you Jews call *God-fearers.*"

"And have you heard of the coming of the Messiah?"

"We have heard of the Messiah, yes. We are waiting for his coming. Over twenty years ago a man named John, called the Immerser, went about Judea announcing that the Messiah would soon come."

"Sirs," Paul asked inquisitively, "did you receive the Holy Spirit when you believed?"

"No," they replied, "we don't know what you mean. We have never heard that there is a Holy Spirit."

Paul smiled. "Brothers, may I sit down with you for a few minutes?"

"By all means" was their ready reply.

Paul went straight to the issue. "The Messiah has come! You have not heard of his death and resurrection? Or the fulfillment of Pentecost and the coming of the Holy Spirit?"

Now it was their turn to be curious. You could see excitement, wonder, and confusion on the faces of all twelve men.

"What is your name?" asked Paul of one of the men.

"My name is Epenetus."

"Where are you from?"

"I am from here, Asia Minor."

(I, Timothy, must tell you that there were six young men watching this unfolding drama with mouths open and eyes wide.)

Paul began to tell the men of the coming of John's cousin, the Messiah. A few minutes later, to our everlasting amaze-

immersed twelve men from Asia Minor into the waters of death and the resurrection—twelve men out of death and into Christ. We were joyful beyond words. No, we were euphoric.

"This is what we were praying about," stammered Epenetus. "That someone would come to us to tell us if the Messiah had come." Although already exhausted from sheer glory, we all began shouting praises to our Lord. We six men were so excited that day that we could have put out the fires of hell with no more than a cup of water.

Paul slipped into the water with us.

"Titus, you brothers have wondered just how we would begin in Ephesus. You have wondered how difficult it would be. See, brothers . . . how easy it is?"

We laughed, we cried, we laughed, and laughed some more.

(Later Paul whispered to me, "*Perhaps*, it will not always be so easy.")

A few minutes later nineteen men walked through the gates of Ephesus while rejoicing, singing, shouting, and addressing the angels. As praise turned to prayer, we made all sorts of declarations to the city of Ephesus, to the principalities and powers and to the Lord. We were not too unlike the man Peter had healed in the Temple in Jerusalem. We were walking and leaping and praising God. I must add that one Paul of Tarsus was making as much an uproar as any of us.

So it was that we came to Ephesus. And so it was, on that same day, we entered the home of a couple who had been awaiting our arrival for many months. And on that day five young men had the honor of meeting Priscilla and Aquila for the first time.

ment, every man there was convicted by the Holy Spirit ar
believed. It was Epenetus who first exclaimed, "Sir, I believe
believe!"

Paul went on to tell the story of what happened after
Crucifixion and Resurrection. In a moment the eleven ot
men followed Epenetus in open confession of the Lord. Be
our very eyes we saw twelve Gentiles receive the life of J
Christ.

"Now brothers, if you would, please kneel and receive
Holy Spirit."

We, the six, standing about twenty feet away, coul
have uttered a word had our lives depended upon it
watched Paul lay hands on twelve men and saw twelve
baptized in the Holy Spirit. As in the home of Cornelius
all spoke in tongues.

Paul turned around and looked straight at us. "You
that in the Jewish ritual of Pentecost there are *two* lo
bread that are placed in the oven. Today, far from Isra
have witnessed the meaning *and* the fulfillment of tha
loaf."

The twelve new believers walked toward us as we
toward them. Perfect strangers put their arms arou
other and rejoiced in Christ Jesus. Someone began a so
happened that all *nineteen* of us knew the song. And so
together as one. After the song ended some of the m
gled to utter their very first prayer to their Lord an
Jesus Christ. It was just too much. I can say with acc
we all lost control of ourselves.

It so happened that the Cayster River was ne
motioned to the six of us and pointed to the river.
later six young men slipped down into the water, e
us still crying profusely. The twelve believers slipp
water with us. Six Gentiles from Syria, Galatia,

CHAPTER 14

Welcome, soldiers," said Priscilla. "But I didn't expect so many of you!"

Those words fired us up, all over again. Finally we became rational enough to explain to Priscilla what had happened. She was soon as overcome as we were.

Aquila, who arrived moments later, kept muttering, "What a beginning—my, my, my, what a beginning!"

To say the least, it was an unprecedented hour for all of us.

That evening we were served a sumptuous meal prepared by the hands of Priscilla. That night we all agreed to meet together again the next evening: a gathering—an *assembly*—of God's people just twenty-four hours after our arrival.

What a beginning it was!

That same day Priscilla and Aquila showed us around their home. It was one of the largest homes inside the walls of the city. The most outstanding feature of the home was a room that could hold perhaps fifty or more people.

Just before dark a weary church planter and his young trainees found their rooms and fell asleep.

As usual, Paul was up before any of us. By the time we awoke he had already joined Aquila in the marketplace, taking the weaver's beam, but stopping now and then to mend a leaky tent or repair a harness.

This was Paul. Whatever city he ventured into, he determined to be a model to the other believers. That first new morning in Ephesus, Paul again took that stewardship for himself. Paul made himself a model for other Christians *and* for future workers. This "model for us" was central to the purpose of Paul's life.

Unlike the men called to work among the Jews, our brother Paul *was never* a full-time Christian worker. Neither was he a *part-time* worker. Paul of Tarsus accomplished all that he did, not as one who worked for the Lord full- or part-time; Paul was a *spare-time* worker in the Lord's ministry. And yet, despite serving the Lord only in his spare time, wherever he trod . . . the earth shook. No full-time worker of our age accomplished more than Paul! Will there ever be such a man as Paul again? May his example live forever, and may others dare follow this high standard.

The day Paul began the Lord's work in Ephesus, he had only twelve years left to live. Paul's thoughts now centered on the coming Sabbath and the synagogue. He knew that Priscilla had made many friends there, and—best of all—Paul had been well received there on a stopover less than a year earlier.

"Old Blastinius might not be quite as smart as he thinks he is," Titus said as we made our way to the synagogue. "His imagination cannot reach as far or as fast as Paul can travel. Priscilla told me that no one here has ever heard a critical word concerning Paul."

The six of us took our places among the God-fearers. Gaius had the ruddy look of a young man from a small country village. Secundus and Aristarchus wore the deeply etched features of Greeks, their eyes black and shiny, their hair as black as a raven, their skin so light it seemed to glow like the sun. Sopater, blond with blue eyes, had not even one inch that looked Jewish. Then there was Titus, who looked very much like an Assyrian from Babylon! Unfortunately, none of my mother's Jewish features had ever reached the surface of my skin. I bore only the image of my father . . . not unlike the features of Secundus and Aristarchus. As we moved to the place where God-fearers were consigned, I remarked teasingly to my five friends, "Be honored to sit with me; I have stepped down from my high state as a Jew to be with you heathen this day."

"It is only that you have less skin than we that you are so illustrious," whispered Titus.

Truthfully, all through the ritual we were six very lighthearted men struggling hard to look pious if not religious.

The Jews sat either on three-legged stools or on the bench that was built onto the synagogue wall. Yet others sat on the floor. Paul and Aquila took their places near the front. Priscilla, grumbling all the while about having to sit through *any* synagogue services, took her place in the balcony.

That Paul was in the company of Aquila (and in his Pharisee garb) gave him instant approval in the eyes of the onlookers. (The elders had heard of Paul's arrival and were anxious to hear from him again.) Aquila and Priscilla had gained great respect in the synagogue. Virtually every person in the room had, at one time or other, been a guest in the home of Priscilla and Aquila.

At the end of the ritual, as expected, Paul was asked to speak. Six men held their breath, for we knew we were going to learn *something*.

Paul began with the story about the ancient Hebrew prediction of a Messiah. But to our amazement, he went all the way back *before* Creation. We were hearing Paul say things *none* of us had ever heard. We were hanging on to his words like men who had *never* heard him speak before! Paul worked his way forward *only* to the time of Creation itself. There he ended his message and sat down. He was immediately invited to return the next Sabbath! As we walked out of the building, we were six awed and elated young men, for *we* had witnessed a Paul we had never heard before.

"Is there no end to the depths of this man?" muttered Titus.

Paul had, once again, done what he had so earnestly committed himself to do: He had gone to the Jews *first*, a custom he continued throughout his entire life. He did so, knowing full well that he would one day be rejected there. It was at that moment that he knew he was free to go to the Gentiles.

A few months later, one of the elders from the synagogue received the inevitable letter warning of Paul's teaching.

The letter was unsigned. Despite that fact, within hours the Jewish elders had met. The next day they were in Aquila's home. Priscilla showed them in. They requested to see Aquila and Paul. Priscilla complied but insisted on being present. When Jewish eyebrows rose, Priscilla replied, "It is *my* home, and I am a *Roman* woman."

Paul sat there, waiting for the inevitable.

The elders spoke only a few words. "Paul, we, the elders of the Ephesian synagogue, ask you not to return to our synagogue."

That was the end of it. The men stood and walked out of Priscilla's home.

"What will you do now, Paul?" wondered Aquila out loud.

Priscilla broke in with her mischievous personality and her honest words. "I tell you what I am going to do; I am going to rejoice that I will *never* have to go back to a boring synagogue again as long as I live!"

Paul's answer was a surprise. "Aquila, it is not what I am going to do, it is what I have already *done.*" Paul gave no further explanation. "Priscilla, may we nineteen continue to meet here? Perhaps *frequently?*"

"Frequently?" said Priscilla, in a voice of protest. "Every morning before dawn and every evening when the sun goes down? *Every* day?"

Priscilla then eyed Paul cautiously. "Paul of Tarsus, I can tell that you have something you are hiding. Not only that, you are *enjoying* hiding it. What is it?"

Paul had hoped someone would ask.

"Remember Corinth?" he said, with obvious delight. "How we were able to rent the home next door to the synagogue?"

Priscilla nodded, then began to laugh! "Not again! Here in Ephesus! Have you rented a place next door to the synagogue, Paul? Why, I am ashamed of you," she said as she clapped her hands in delight. "You have? You *are!* You are going to try to do the same thing here!"

"No, I'm not going to *try* to do the same thing. I have already done it."

Priscilla let out a squeal.

"Tyrannus teaches in his school from dawn until just before noon, closing his school at the same time the agora closes. During the time everyone leaves the market and goes home to rest, I have the use of his building. Tyrannus does not use his school during the afternoon when the market is closed."

"*Every* afternoon I have the building. Can I help it if his school happens to be next door to the synagogue?"

Aquila's brow furrowed. "Tell me, Paul, has anyone ever accused you of being *subtle?*" Priscilla was laughing and kicking her feet in sheer delight.

"This is my hope, Aquila. You and I will awaken the dawn and work in the market until time for the noon meal. (From time to time I will lay aside my work and speak in the marketplace.) At noon we will close our shop. I will then go to Tyrannus's school and spend the next three or four hours with the six young men who are here with me. On most occasions the schoolroom will be open to everyone, so that those who desire may come and listen. Of course, there will be times I will close the doors to have private meetings just with the six."

"Excellent! But Paul, you need not work at all."

"Actually, Aquila, I *must.* It is up to me alone to supply all the needs of these six young men. I must labor not only for my own needs but also for those of these young men."

"And when do you propose to rest, Paul of Tarsus?" asked Priscilla.

"Every time there is a heathen holiday! And there are many of those."

"No, you will not," jabbed Priscilla. "I never saw a heathen holiday pass but that you spent every minute of it with the assembly."

"True, Paul, true," agreed Aquila.

Paul was not really listening, as was often the case when he was confronted with a call to take care of himself. "This is probably my last opportunity to ever train young men. Everything I have heard about the happenings in Israel is foreboding. And, as you can see, Blastinius is closing the doors of synagogues *everywhere.* I am no longer a young man; you might even call me old. My time is limited. Perhaps short. *This* is *my* time. I would not have wanted to train men until now; but *now* is that time, and I must make every moment count."

(I, Timothy, write these words to you many years after "the Ephesian hour." I was a young man then. Today, as I write, I am old. I must agree with what Paul said that day. Only men who have been church planters and only men who are old should train young men to be church planters. The reason is simple. It takes a lifetime before one is qualified to do *this*—the highest work of all.)

Even though the synagogue was closed to Paul that day, many in the synagogue had already turned to the Lord. Many more than just nineteen of us would gather in Priscilla's home.

That evening after dark Paul presented to the six of us his plan concerning Tyrannus's house. We howled with delight. Four hours with Paul, *every* day.

When we were not at Tyrannus's school, we spent our time on things Paul gave us to do. And in prayer. Paul promised that we would be the busiest men in Ephesus, and he kept his word. Paul was unrelenting in his expectations of us. And we loved *almost* every minute of it.

"Whenever I go into the marketplace to preach, I will let you know, for I want you to be there. One day I will ask each of you to speak there. Nor will I give you any advance notice. None. You must all be prepared to speak for Christ, instantly.

"You shall pursue the presence of Jesus Christ above all else—this is your first priority." Paul's eyes flashed, his jaw fixed as he spoke. "The school of Tyrannus will be for you what Solomon's Colonnade was for Barnabas, Stephen, Silas, Philip, Agabus, and others when they went there with the Twelve. Remember, too, that visitors will be coming to many of these meetings. Most will be brothers and sisters in the ecclesia, but some will be men and women coming here from other cities; still others will be there out of curiosity. Sometimes I will speak directly to them. When I do, listen."

Paul drew in a deep breath and added, "Do not think that our entire time will be sitting in Tyrannus's school. I plan to *send* you out to surrounding cities. As Jesus sent out the Twelve, so I will send you out. In his case, it was for no more than two weeks. But for you . . . later . . . as God allows, you may expect to be gone for weeks. Perhaps months."

"Why would you do that when the Lord sent out the Twelve for only a few days?" asked Sopater.

Paul shot back, "Because you have received the Holy Spirit!

They had not, not at that time. The Holy Spirit *in* you . . . that is something the disciples did not have until the day of the Resurrection, when the risen Lord breathed on them. Jesus Christ dwells in you, now!

There is another reason. You have lived in the ecclesia of God for years. In these two ways you are ahead of the Twelve at the time Jesus was training them. You are far more prepared at this point in your life to come to know the Lord intimately and to experience his indwelling Spirit than the Twelve were during the three years the Lord lived with them. The Holy Spirit was not *in* them at that time. Nor *on* them. Nor had the church been born."

A hush fell over us. I, Timothy, can say from that time on I was not quite as envious of the Twelve as I had been. In some ways the training we received was beyond that which the Twelve received. Calvary was behind us; the Resurrection was behind us and built into us. Besides that, the coming of the Holy Spirit was behind us. All that the Lord accomplished in those *three* great events was *now* working, moving, and operating inside us! And, praise God, all six of us had lived in the experience of the church of Jesus Christ.

It is important that I tell you of the first time we gathered in Tyrannus's house. We all remember well what Paul said to us that day.

CHAPTER 15

The Lord Jesus Christ has sent me to be a model," Paul began, "a model to the church, a model of what a church planter ought to be, a model to you as future workers, *and* just as important, a model as to how one trains new workers. Watch everything I do. Watch everything I say. Listen to my every word, no matter how small it is nor how large. It matters not if it is something spiritual or if it is something practical. Whether it be a command or a comment, watch my life. Watch my life.

"What we do in Ephesus will be unprecedented in all history, except for those three years in Galilee. You will not be trained as the Greeks train. I am *not* Aristotle, and this is not a classroom!

"It is important that you notice how many times I rebuke someone. Count the number! Notice how often I give a command. Count! Notice how often I criticize either the individual or the church. Count! Notice how often I correct. Count how often I confront a brother for something he has done wrong. Keep record! Then, for all your life remember that you should do such things no more often than I have. And if you will keep a count of the times that I do anything or say anything negative to brothers and sisters, you will surely do almost no correcting for as long as you live."

Paul's eyes sparkled! "But do *not* count how many times I do these things to you six. I have plans to place every one of you under the stricter standards and then bury you!"

We laughed nervously.

"Watch me. There is always a way other than criticizing and correcting. There are ways other than being negative. May God extend to you the grace to see these things in my life as I work among the holy ones—both with the ecclesia *and* with individuals.

"It is very difficult to define *bearing the cross.* It is better to learn this by watching. Also, notice how much I complain. Notice how often I am angry with God or his people. Watch and see how often I ask the Lord to explain to me what it is he is doing. If someone is healed, watch, not so much how I do it but how much attention I draw to a healing. The same is true of signs, wonders, and deliverance."

Those were Paul's opening words! And if we had stopped right then, we would have already been changed men.

Then, almost in anger, Paul added, "You will have little or no excuse to ever put someone under guilt. You will have little or no reason to rebuke. Or to show anger. These are not tools for you to use lightly. You should suffer long and hard before you ever turn to anything negative. If necessary, lose, lose *everything* before picking up old, useless, worn-out tools of rebuke, chastising, disciplining the wrongdoer, confrontation, and other such kin—these tools destroy believers. They *do not* build up! A situation must be dire beyond all telling before you become one who corrects the church of Jesus Christ or a member of his body. She is his *bride*, *remember* that!

"Treat her as a bride.

"I told you that some men who wanted to be chosen to be trained became angry when *not* chosen. One or two have left the church and are very bitter. Shall you be of such low quality?"

Then, as though he had not said enough to frighten us, he

added, "I have one more thing to say to you. Never be pretentious. Never look like a Pharisee, never look like a Sadducee, never look like a scribe, and never look like a priest. You should always earn your living. As to dress, you should look like a man who earns his living. Wear what is *typically* worn in the marketplace. Never pretend to be pious, never pretend to be spiritual, and never pretend you are religious. You are, and forever shall be, nothing but a brother!"

Six young men swallowed hard. One of us began to weep. (As I recall, I think it was Gaius.) Then we all gathered around Paul and began to pray. Then we wept. At that very moment, though we had only been together for a few minutes, the tenor was set for the next three years. There, down on our faces, we implored our Lord concerning the things Paul had just said to us. Looking back, I believe we were faithful to the commitment we made that day . . . that is, as faithful as fallen men can be.

As Paul expected, many came in from other cities to be in that room with us. Some curious. A few, confrontational. Everything that happened in Ephesus during those next three years had a profound effect on towns all over that small province called Asia Minor. Paul sent us out to those cities. And we came back just as the Twelve did, to learn at the feet of the one who sent us out.

There was one event that happened later that changed the course of the lives of all six of us. It is the story of the conversion of two young men, blood brothers. And . . . well . . . it happened one evening in Priscilla's home.

CHAPTER 16

It was one of the most glorious meetings ever held in Priscilla's home. Perhaps one of the most glorious meetings any of us ever attended. Everything about that meeting had been pure glory. Beyond that, there were two young men who had come into the room. They were there to *see.* They sat down quietly at the back of the room. They were both every inch Greeks. At first they looked a bit lost in such unusual surroundings—but, oh, the meeting itself was sublime. It would have won the heart of anyone. The presence of the Lord was there in all his beauty.

We must have sung twenty, perhaps thirty, or more songs. Interspersed between them were prayers and words of testimony brought by brothers and sisters. Among those who spoke were several new believers who told what it was like encountering a living Christ. A number of slaves expressed the joy of working with other slaves who had become believers. They expressed how *free* they were. "I'm free," said one slave, "in here!" as he pointed to his heart. Everyone in the room was simply sitting there absorbing the glory of the Lord's Spirit as he moved in the assembly.

Out of the corner of my eye, I was watching the two young men. One of them stood.

"May I ask a question?"

Smiles and reassurances met him from all sides.

"I know some of you. A few of you are my friends. Many of you have come to this place and then told me of one who died for me and who rose again from the dead. You have said he lives inside you. I cannot see this one, but I can *feel* him.

"Right now I feel that *someone* whom I cannot see is calling me. I do not understand anything except this: I do not wish to ever leave this room—not tonight, not tomorrow, not ever. I wish to stay here forever and ever and never leave."

The young man began to weep.

Such was our introduction to Trophimus.

Gaining control of himself, he looked up and asked, "Is there anything I am supposed to do, any creed I am supposed to know, anything I am supposed to learn?"

There was a titter of laughter across the room, accompanied by knowing smiles. Others, upon first coming to the ecclesia, had also wondered the same things. A brother on the other side of the room stood.

"A few weeks ago I came into this room, and I had the same questions. Now I can answer your questions. Yes, there is a creed. Yes, there is something to know. And, yes, there is something to do. But it really isn't something, it's *someone*. The creed is Jesus Christ; the one to know is Jesus Christ. And there is something to do: Believe on Jesus Christ with all your heart."

"How may I know him?"

I, Timothy, am sure that there was someone in the room who was about to answer. Instead, a sister began to sing. The song and the words were perfect. It was a simple song, with a beautiful melody, about the Lord Jesus.

Trophimus began to weep again. His brother, Tychicus, stood up and put his arms around Trophimus. The song began again. By now the crying had spread all over the room. Once more the song began. This time Trophimus and Tychicus joined in. And again the song was sung. Trophimus and Tychicus began speaking the words of the song directly to the Lord.

The song was sung for the final time. The entire house was filled with joyful weeping. Everyone gathered around Tychicus and Trophimus, and, as they so often do, they simply pressed in around one another and then touched the two young men. Words of encouragement were spoken to each of them, and every time someone spoke, everyone began weeping all over again.

Then the song began again. It was pure glory. A few moments later the quiet voice of Priscilla was heard. "Brothers, take these men out to the river and immerse them into Christ."

The two young Greeks had no idea what that meant, but they embraced one another—so much so that I feared for both of them. A moment later everyone poured out the doorway into the street. Together we walked down the narrow Ephesian lanes, then out of the city and into the countryside until we came again to the banks of the Cayster River.

"We come here often, it seems, does it not?" whispered Gaius.

Paul sat down on the riverbank, a soft glow on his face. Titus and I sat down beside him. "I think that I am going to see a great deal more of these men," said Paul.

Three of the brothers in the ecclesia (all slaves) stepped out into the water, followed by the two young Greeks. There Tychicus and Trophimus were immersed into the waters of death and raised up again, living witnesses to the resurrection of Christ and the newness of the Life that beat within them. About half the believers slipped into the water, while all laughed and rejoiced. We were there at least another hour, exhorting, encouraging, testifying, and singing to these two new brothers.

In the days ahead Paul's words proved to be correct. We saw these two young men *every* day in the meetings and *every* day in the schoolroom. Since then I have seen those two men in cities all over the Roman Empire! I have seen Tychicus and Trophimus in Jerusalem. I have seen them in Rome. (One day, in Jerusalem, one of them almost got Paul killed. But that is another story.)

And, if you think this was glorious, let me tell you of the young man from Colosse. (You have heard of him.) The first time I saw him he was my age. He grew up to be a giant in the Lord Jesus Christ. He was, perhaps, the best of us all.

CHAPTER 17

The man I speak of was from Colosse, a small town ninety miles east of Ephesus. But before you meet him, you must first meet another citizen of Colosse.

It was about the time for the noon meal when an elderly man walked into Tyrannus's school. "My name is Philemon. I am from the city of Colosse. I have been listening to you in the marketplace."

Paul nodded. "Come in."

"I wish to believe."

"Explain."

"I believe the Messiah has come. And I believe he has come, not just for the Jews, but for me and for all the heathen. I believe his name is Jesus Christ and that this Jesus died for me. I believe he can cleanse me from my sins. And . . . and . . . live in me."

It is probable that Paul did not know exactly how to respond to so simple and so beautiful a word. What Paul answered was so fitting: "Philemon, it seems to me that you have already believed."

Philemon began to shake. Then, to cry. As one, all six of us stood and gathered around the stranger. The rest of the day

Paul laid aside everything to listen to this man tell his story, responding when necessary. The shadows of night had fallen across the city before we left the room.

It is important that you know more about Philemon. (A letter Paul wrote to him years later has been copied and read all over the empire.) Philemon comes from a town that is part of a triangle of three cities. The other two cities in the triangle are Hierapolis and Laodicea, all of them being about ten miles apart.

Philemon traded in fleece, as the Colossian fleece is some of the most sought after in all the world. It happened that Philemon came to Ephesus often to buy and to sell. But on this occasion, Philemon had also come to purchase a slave in the slave market. While in the marketplace he heard Paul speak. After believing in Christ, Philemon decided to spend as long a time in Ephesus as possible before returning to his home city. Having made that decision, Philemon joined us in all of our meetings as well as the meetings of the church. He never missed anything. The rest of the time Philemon sat at the feet of Paul in the marketplace, simply listening.

The day inevitably came when Philemon had to return home to Colosse, but not before he had purchased a slave, about sixteen years old. On the day he purchased this young man he remarked, "Because most slaves are dead by the time they are twenty-five, I hope I have made a profitable decision." From that comment came the slave's name, Onesimus, which in Greek means "profitable."

Onesimus was the son of a Germanic barbarian whose family had been captured by Romans during one of the frequent wars on the northern border of the Roman Empire. Onesimus was truly Germanic, for he was as white as white can be. His eyes were a deep blue, and he looked nothing like any people living within the boundaries of the Roman Empire.

On his last day in Ephesus, Philemon brought Onesimus to the gathering of the assembly. He simply sat passively, his Germanic mind understanding not one word he heard that day. Onesimus was simply a frightened boy interested in nothing. His kind was looked upon as savage, and truly he was barbarian.

When Paul asked one of the brothers, who was himself a slave, the state of Onesimus's soul, the brother pointed to his own heart and said, "I believe Onesimus is not yet free."

Upon his departure, Philemon said to Paul, "I am in debt to you forever, my brother. I owe you my life. I implore you to come to Colosse and bring us the gospel. A room in my house will be reserved for you . . . forever! When you come, bring us an ecclesia, an assembly, like the one that gathers here in Ephesus. I know that without the church I will never fully come to know the joy of having received Jesus Christ."

"Perhaps I will come," responded Paul, "or I may send someone else. In the meantime, Philemon, when you return home, tell all your friends what has happened to you here."

Return he did, and he told his many friends. Still, we could never have imagined the response of one of those friends.

Some months after Philemon left Ephesus, a tall young man came into the marketplace, found Paul, stood right in front of him, and listened as one transfixed. The next day this strange young man was back in the marketplace again, standing before Paul, never once moving. The following day, just as we had come into the school of Tyrannus for the afternoon, this young man walked in. The men in that room would soon come to love this Colossian as much as anyone in this world.

I shall never forget that moment. When he came through the door, he almost filled the entire doorway. He stopped just behind me, then, looking straight into Paul's eyes, he said, "I have come to be baptized."

None of us had ever heard anyone doing anything exactly

like that before. A perfect stranger had walked into the room and had come straight to the point.

Paul looked up at the young man with eyes as intense as his and said, "Upon what grounds would you be immersed into Christ?"

There was no hesitation in the young man's voice. "My home is in Colosse. A man named Philemon has told me of Jesus Christ. This Christ I have received. I have walked to Ephesus; I have listened to you in the marketplace. For the last two nights I have slept in the streets, speaking to this Lord. I have waited, but I can wait no longer. Jesus Christ lives inside me. Sometimes I feel that he will break the ribs of my chest."

I, Timothy, did not know whether to laugh or to cry or to jump up and down. But this I can tell you, that day I met a giant in the kingdom of God, for upon that day I met the one, the only, Epaphras.

He added one other sentence. "I am in Christ, and Christ is in me. Please find a place where there is water so that I may show everyone that I am Christ's."

Paul stood up and walked over to the young man and answered strength with strength. "What is your name?"

"I am Epaphras, a friend of Philemon, and I wish to be immersed. If you will let me, I would like to stay here in your city as long as possible to sit in the assembly. Philemon told me that my brothers and sisters gather in the home of one named Aquila."

Epaphras looked down at Paul as intently as any man I have ever seen and added, "You cannot deny me the privilege of meeting in the assembly, and you cannot deny me immersion for I have found Christ." I watched Paul do something I had rarely seen him do. He began to laugh and cry at the same time. He could not speak.

But Aristarchus could. "Brother Epaphras, upon your

confession, made with your own mouth, that you believe that the Lord Jesus Christ has saved you, I will take you at this very moment to the closest water we can find and there plunge you into the waters of death and watch as you rise to resurrection and life in Jesus Christ."

Sopater stood. "And I am ready to help him do so."

We did not return to Tyrannus's school that day. Together we marched to the river. Epaphras did not ask so much as a single question. He boldly walked into the water, raising both hands to the skies and his face to the heavens. *Then* he spoke. He had a voice that seemed to sound its way across creation.

"Take me into your death, my dear Lord. Then, by your good mercies, raise me up with you!"

I was looking upon the face of someone who was going to stretch the boundaries of devotion to Jesus Christ. Neither I, nor Paul, nor anyone else has ever met the equal of this young man named Epaphras.

With shouts ringing out across the water, Aristarchus and Sopater took our new friend and slipped him into the waters of the Cayster River. When he came up out of the waters, we were treated to shouts, admonitions, adulation, and exhortations, the likes of which we had never before heard. Standing there in the middle of that water, dripping wet, that young man preached Jesus Christ to all of us. We began to laugh and to cry, and then we shouted in unison with his exhortations. I laughed until I hurt. All the while Epaphras, oblivious to us all, continued his declarations. He stood there, waist deep in water, proclaiming the glories of Christ.

I turned to Paul. "It seems that Philemon has been a good teacher."

"Perhaps we should invite Philemon back to Ephesus and sit at *his* feet and there learn from *him*," Paul responded.

The next morning Epaphras had found work in the marketplace; by nightfall he had moved in with some of the brothers. He would live with us for almost a year. To my knowledge, except when work necessitated it, Epaphras never missed a meeting of the ecclesia or the gathering in Tyrannus's school, always earning his own keep. He never spoke a negative word to anyone about anything, nor did I ever hear him complain. In the meetings in Tyrannus's school Epaphras seemed to have a perception of Christ and of things spiritual and invisible, which the rest of us simply did not possess.

The day Epaphras returned home to Colosse, he left a great empty place in all our lives. It was as though one of the six had departed. It is with great pride that today, so many years later, I can say to you that it was my privilege to have worked side by side with Epaphras for many years. He came the closest to being another Paul as any man I have ever known.

Many came to Ephesus, as did Philemon, from towns and cities around Ephesus. They returned to tell their friends and families about the ecclesia in Ephesus.

Not even Paul had anticipated the results of this word-of-mouth testimony about Jesus Christ.

The Lord was preparing the way for the ecclesia of Christ to be planted in cities throughout all of Asia Minor. Before we departed Ephesus, there was hardly a place in Asia Minor but one of us had visited it. In most cases a gathering had come into being, all because men and women who had visited Ephesus had returned to their homes talking of Christ. Every town in Asia Minor had at least one or two families who belonged to Christ and who were imploring us to come and proclaim Christ in their city.

So much happened in Ephesus during those three years that the results are still reverberating throughout the empire. The fruit of Ephesus continues to this very day. I doubt I have lived a year since then but I have met someone who found

Christ in Ephesus and who later became an instrument in carrying the gospel of Christ to a new place.

Now I, Timothy, must tell you what happened to Tychicus and Trophimus.

CHAPTER 18

One morning Paul took the six of us aside. "These two men, Tychicus and Trophimus, have been with us in Ephesus almost from the beginning. Both say they have been called to the Lord's work. I am usually very skeptical when I hear someone say this, but I can find no reason to doubt that confession. I find these two brothers to be steadfast men. Perhaps they will fall by the wayside in as far as being workers—but perhaps not. Time will tell."

Paul then studied each of our faces. "In fact, there is no guarantee about any of you!

"Where will any of you be in five years? Perhaps all of you will be serving the Lord—perhaps none of you. It is a risky thing to be serving the Lord; it is a thing difficult beyond description, and there is discouragement beyond knowing. So many who think they want to serve the Lord also think that men and women will follow what they have to say. Be assured, young men, this will rarely happen.

"Nonetheless, I wish to ask you, what is your sense about adding these men to your number? What is your judgment on this matter?"

We were, at first, surprised. That is, surprised that Paul would place the decision in our hands. Gaius responded, "May we go outside and discuss this?"

"Perhaps we will need a day to consider this," added Titus.

There was a catch in Aristarchus's voice when he said, "I only wish that Epaphras could be with us right now." Every head nodded in agreement.

A moment later the six of us stepped out into the street and huddled into a small circle. We began to pray. One or two questions were raised, and clear answers were given.

Sopater spoke for us all. "Not one of us has the right to be here."

Secundus then added, "They look every bit as qualified as I do!" To this we all gave a strong *amen!*

"Their devotion to Christ is as strong as any of ours. But as to their call?"

Then Aristarchus added, "There are six men standing here from five different provinces. Each day we sit at Paul's feet. It seems fitting to me that someone from Asia Minor should be sitting at his feet. An Ephesian! Let us believe."

"Brothers, we do not need to wait until tomorrow," announced Titus. "We are all in agreement. Let's ask Paul to invite these two young men to join our number, immediately."

"Eight instead of six," said Sopater.

As we turned back into the school, Paul met us at the door.

"We all have the same mind, Paul. We would like to ask you to invite Tychicus and . . . "

"Me?" rejoined Paul. "Absolutely not. This is for you to do. It is your decision—you do the inviting."

"But Paul, do you approve?" asked Gaius.

"Was I not the one who brought up the subject?" responded Paul wryly.

And so from that day on, there were no longer six of us being trained, but eight. And each one wished that Epaphras could have made it nine.

As to Epaphras, he seemed to have disappeared from our

lives. There were rumors about him from time to time. One thing we knew for certain: Wherever he was, he was proclaiming Jesus Christ. We felt certain that many would respond to his message. I felt certain that one day we would see that brother again.

We had been in Ephesus for a little less than a year when Paul unexpectedly received a letter from Barnabas. It was with the receiving of that letter that things began to move very rapidly in all our lives.

CHAPTER 19

A letter from Barnabas. Titus, you read it aloud to all of us."

As Titus read, Paul listened intently. When Titus finished, Paul looked up and said, "The world is shifting under our feet. Things are changing in the empire by the day. The enormity of what is happening is beyond our ability to grasp."

Paul looked at the last words of the letter. "I see that Barnabas has come to signing his name in very large letters, just as I do.

"In all this letter, so full of dastardly news, is one wonderful word: Corinth! At last Peter is going to visit Corinth! Peter—in Greece. Imagine it! With Barnabas at his side!

"I have always hoped that Peter would visit at least one of the Gentile churches that have come from my hand. It is important—important to the future unity of the churches. There is no better choice than Corinth, as there are so many Jews in the assembly there.

"Nonetheless, I admire his courage. Peter knows he is risking the wrath of the Daggermen if he—of all Jews—visits an assembly of the uncircumcised.

"Here, Titus, read this part again."

Titus looked at the place where Paul was pointing, smiled, and read again Barnabas's words.

"John Mark has asked that I tell Timothy and Titus that he and Peter are working together on a brief story of the Lord's life."

I said nothing but threw one hand in the air in exhilaration. Titus did the same.

Once more Paul, having squinted at the words, handed the letter to Titus. "Read this part again."

"I have asked Peter to visit Cyprus. Peter is also determined to go to North Africa. The situation in Jerusalem is drastic. The emperor Claudius has appointed a *Gentile* as governor of Israel. The one appointed is a man who has no sympathy with, nor understanding of, the Jewish people. Roman soldiers have insulted, desecrated, and blasphemed the Temple."

Paul broke in. "Just recently an envoy of Jewish leaders went to Caesarea-by-the-Sea to talk with the new proconsul about these constant insults to Israel. No good resulted from their visit. Continue with the letter."

"One of the worst things that has happened here in Israel of late is that some Samaritans killed a Hebrew. This crime was brought before the governor, Cumanus, who did nothing about it. A delegation of Jews was then sent to Caesarea. Again, Cumanus refused to do anything about the killing of a Jew. This incensed all of Israel. As a result, a man named Eleazar Ben Dinai raised up a small army, crossed over into Samaria, and burned down several villages in Samaria.

"As long as Cumanus was governor, he remained disinterested in what was happening in Israel. As a result, several secret societies have recently grown up. All have one common goal, the purification of the Jewish religion.

"The most dangerous of the secret societies is still the *sicarii*—the Daggermen. They are country people. They first choose their victim, then come into Jerusalem at festival times and work their way through the crowd until they come upon the one whom they feel is undermining the law of Moses. They then stab the man with a small dagger, move back, and join the rest of the crowd in indignation at such a terrible assassination. None have been caught. No one seems to know the identity of any of these men.

"When Cumanus was replaced, the emperor once more did something very unwise. He appointed a man named Felix to be the new governor. Felix was once a slave! A former military commander, he is the first military man ever to be appointed to govern Israel. This appointment is almost a declaration of war. In all of Roman history no military man has ever been appointed as governor of any country or province. Just after Felix became governor, he captured Eleazar Ben Dinai and had him executed. Felix's understanding of the Israeli people is nonexistent. Nor, I am told, does he have any interest in learning anything about us.

"Beyond that, Israel has had its taxes increased . . . by both Rome and by our own government. Crops in Israel have been poor this year. The loss of food has been very hard on the poor, adding more to the unrest."

For a moment, we saw agony appear on Paul's face. "Sometimes I wonder about the sanity of men in government. In the midst of all these problems that Barnabas has recounted, other news has reached me that the elders of the city of Jerusalem have decided to complete the temple of Herod the Great. They have hired eighteen thousand men to work on the temple. To do this, our ever so wise leaders have levied a new tax! A tax on a people who are on the verge of revolt and suffering from a year of poor crops."

Then, with the keenest of insight, Paul continued, "This is not the first time that a large number of Jews have been hired to work on the temple. I wonder if the Jewish leaders remember what happened the last time? Jerusalem suddenly ran out of money and had to tell thousands of men that they would no longer be paid. The work on the temple came to a halt. But worse, suddenly thousands of men had no work and no money. That fact almost brought on a national riot. If one day those eighteen thousand men are told that they will no longer be paid, that in itself will start a revolution.

"Do not misunderstand the gravity of the situation. The majority of the people in Israel favor a revolt against Rome, but the reason they give is insane. They believe that if they revolt, a Messiah will immediately appear out of nowhere and deliver them from Rome either by the sword or by some kind of heavenly intervention, such as striking all the Romans dead.

"Right now there are strong feelings in the countryside, where the suffering is greatest, against the wealthy Jews in the large cities. Those who make their living off Rome are the ones the *sicarii* are after.

"Recently, the *sicarii* have turned their attention to killing not only those who gained their wealth from Rome but to others—like *Peter*—whom they see as a threat to the law of Moses. The believers in the ecclesia in Jerusalem fear the Daggermen may decide that Peter should be assassinated."

Paul's next sentence came very heavily. "The church in Jerusalem has asked Peter to leave Israel for his safety.

"Please read the next words, brother Titus."

"I, Barnabas, am writing this letter at the request of Peter that you might know what is going on in Israel. Peter plans to leave Israel soon to travel to North Africa, specifically to the city of Alexandria."

Once more Paul interrupted. "Peter and I discussed North Africa at length. We both believe that whatever work begins there, Jews and Gentiles working together should do it. For that reason he is taking several Gentiles with him to Alexandria. I could not be more pleased.

"No one can know how grateful I am that Peter has also

decided to come to Corinth by way of Cyprus. He is a man of great integrity. He goes to North Africa with the Gentiles. He travels to Cyprus to help the older churches open themselves to the Gentiles. He then sails to Corinth to speak to both the circumcised and the uncircumcised.

"Titus, now please find the part of the letter that has to do with Blastinius."

We all leaned forward.

"There are many in Jerusalem, even in the church, who follow Blastinius. Some are so angry that Gentiles are being allowed to hear the gospel of Christ that they have denied the faith. Others have not gone so far as that but are in strong disagreement with Peter. There are a large number of Pharisees and scribes in the Jerusalem ecclesia who now listen to Blastinius more than to anyone else.

"I need not tell you, Paul, that Blastinius has written letters to many synagogues warning them of you. Israel is rife with rumors that you have both renounced and denounced Moses and that you have also renounced the festivals and all the ordinances. The letter you wrote to the four Galatian churches has been copied over and over again and has been passed out all over Israel. Reading this letter has created many enemies for you, Paul. There are hundreds who are outraged at your words. There is even a parable that has grown up in Israel concerning you. There are four words to it: *Is Paul a Jew?*"

Once more Paul indicated he wanted to say something. "Up until now Blastinius has been writing letters to synagogues in the Gentile world. Recently he has been writing letters to synagogues and to religious leaders all over Israel. All his letters are about *me.*"

Paul looked up. "My dear eight Gentile brothers, in Israel there is much anger against Peter and myself. Also, because of Claudius's edict against the Jews, there are strong feelings among the Gentiles—everywhere—against the Jews. I do not see how this situation can do anything but get worse."

Titus picked out a sentence in the letter and read it aloud: "The Daggermen grow more hostile toward you every day. The evil things said against you are believed. Like Peter's, your life may soon be in danger, even though you are far away in Asia Minor."

"According to Barnabas's letter," added Titus, "Peter has been quoting the Lord's words about the armies of the Gentiles surrounding Jerusalem: 'When the armies surround Jerusalem, flee! Let those who are on the tops of houses not come down, but flee immediately.'"

"Obviously, Peter is concerned about Israel's future, even its survival," said Paul. "Right now he is beset on every side by his fellow countrymen."

"Here are Barnabas's final words," said Titus: "Paul, you were correct in your view of Cyprus. The Jewish churches on Cyprus do not change. But I have preached Christ to the Gentiles in the cities and towns where there are no Jewish gatherings. These new churches are vibrant and *very* Gentile. It is in going to Cyprus that Peter hopes to bring these two peoples together, as one, in *all* the places where believers assemble."

"Barnabas's letter ends with a traditional Jewish greeting," added Titus. "And, yes, Barnabas's signature is in very large letters, just like yours."

"Well, Barnabas," observed Paul. "It looks as though we have a Pandora's box of problems. I now feel certain that Israel will clash with her oppressors. The Romans are tired of the Hebrews; the Hebrews are tired of the Romans.

"And from all that I have heard, both are tired of Claudius," mused Paul. "I must respond to Barnabas." Paul's eyes glistened. "Peter to Cyprus. Then . . . Peter to Corinth. The news, as concerns the kingdom of God, is good!"

Secundus leaned toward Paul. "Brother, I am not sure you paid attention to everything that is in that letter. You are in increasingly great danger."

"I cannot blame those zealous men, not under the circumstances. I have been zealous for my religion. But I will do this," he said, reflectively. "At the next opportunity I will go to Jerusalem to find a way to demonstrate to them that I am still a Jew."

"I think I see another shaved head," I said.

"Better a shaved one than a missing one," added Titus.

"There is another bright spot in all this," observed Paul. "Since Peter is going to Corinth, I cannot help but think of what wonders will come of that!"

Paul would not wait long to find out what wonders did occur in Corinth. He was laboring in the marketplace when the news reached him.

CHAPTER 20

Peter is in Corinth!"

Paul looked up from his work. It was Sebastian, of the House of Chloe. (The House of Chloe is an ancient trading company that buys, sells, and trades all over the Mediterranean. Its owners are located in Corinth. Sebastian, a slave, is one of their most trusted servants. He comes often to Ephesus from Corinth to buy and sell.)

"Peter has visited us in Corinth."

"I can't believe it," exclaimed Paul, as he embraced Sebastian. "Tell me everything! When did he arrive? Is he still there? How did the assembly receive him?"

"He arrived by ship, from Cyprus, just a few days ago. His wife was with him. So was Barnabas. But they could not stay long—only three days. It seems that Peter was bound for Alexandria. Ships out of Corinth for Egypt are rare. Peter had to take the only available ship, and it was sailing almost immediately. But it was an incredible three days." Sebastian rolled his eyes toward heaven as he spoke.

Paul was beaming.

"Just about everyone in the Corinthian ecclesia went down to Cenchrea to greet Peter at the docks. They then escorted him to Corinth, singing and shouting the entire five miles. Peter was overjoyed. It was three days of jubilation.

"Peter spoke every evening and morning and once in the marketplace. His last gathering with the ecclesia lasted far into the night. He told us so much. He also healed many—and what a sight! For two days he stood in the fields outside the city praying over the sick and infirm.

"On the day Peter departed, not only did the brothers and sisters see him off, but so did hundreds of others. The port of Lechaeum, from which he sailed, was crowded with those who had brought the sick and lame to him. The captain delayed the departure of his ship to give Peter time to lay hands on them."

"Then he was well received in every way!"

"He was! And poor Barnabas—we hardly knew he was there."

"That would be the way Barnabas would want it," replied Paul. "What else?"

"Well, the Hebrews believers were ecstatic, thrilled beyond words!"

"I know. You do not have to tell me. Odd, is it not, that of all the people on earth we Hebrews want to see signs and wonders in order to prove that there is a God?" Paul laughed at his own words.

"The Greeks?"

"They loved him. But word recently came to us that Apollos is returning from Alexandria and will soon arrive in Corinth. The Greeks are as excited about the coming of Apollos as the Jews were at the coming of Peter."

"I understand that, too!" replied Paul, as he threw up his hands in dismay.

"Oh yes, I am supposed to tell you that Apollos may come to you here in Asia Minor after leaving Corinth."

"Excellent," said Paul. "I have never met him. It would be good to have him in Ephesus."

The only other news Sebastian brought was not really news at all. Tension toward Israel was running high in Rome. Rumors were everywhere. The city of Corinth was trying to ignore the issue. After all, the coming of so many Jews to Corinth had proved to be very lucrative for the Corinthians' coffers.

That night Sebastian reported to the gathering in Ephesus. As always, his stay in Ephesus was brief; within a day or two Sebastian had returned to Corinth. But another day would come when Paul of Tarsus would hear from Sebastian—of the House of Chloe—and on that occasion Sebastian would bring some of the worst news Paul would ever hear.

Not long after Sebastian returned to Corinth, the man Apollos arrived in Corinth.

(And, yes, Apollos later came to Ephesus but not to minister. When Apollos came to Ephesus, it was to apologize to Paul for the great harm he had caused in Corinth.)

Now I must tell you of other news—news so astounding that it shook the entire empire. (Paul called it the *best* news to come out of Rome he had ever heard.) It was news so earth-shattering that sailors on board the first ship coming from Rome were shouting it out even before the ship docked at the Ephesian port.

The news?

CHAPTER 21

Claudius is dead! Claudius is dead!" the sailors shouted.

One of the believers working on the dock, a slave, ran into the city to tell Paul. He burst into Priscilla's home yelling, "Claudius is dead, Claudius is dead!"

Paul jumped to his feet. "Are you certain?" were his first words. "Do not tell me news like that unless you are certain."

"Absolutely!" came the answer. "He died no more than seven or eight days ago. The first ship to arrive from Rome since he died just entered the harbor."

"How did he die?" asked Aquila.

"The rumor is that his wife, Agrippina, poisoned him with mushrooms."

"I think I know why," said Priscilla, who was just entering the room.

"What?" said Paul.

"Agrippina is the sister of the late emperor Caligula. When she married Claudius, she already had a son by an earlier marriage. Claudius took this boy, who is about seventeen, as his own son. Then he announced that the boy would become emperor when he died."

"But that's no motive for killing!" said Aquila.

"I heard that Claudius had broken his promise to

Agrippina. After living with her for a while, he began to see the traits of mad Caligula in her. He has been speaking of declaring his own son, Britannicus, the next emperor."

"How do you know this?" asked a mystified Paul.

"I know just about everything going on in Caesar's palace," she announced coolly. "And if you knew Agrippina, you would know why Claudius has grown to fear her. You would also know she could not endure the thought of anyone on the throne except her son. Agrippina has the same diabolical blood in her veins as did her brother, that mad man Caligula. Before Agrippina was the wife of Claudius, she had been the wife of Gnaeus Domitius Ahenobarbus. The son is his. She has burned to see her son emperor," explained Priscilla. "She would stop at *nothing* to fulfill her ambition.

"Just last year, I am told, Claudius insisted that the boy, then sixteen, marry Claudius's daughter Octavia. At that time the boy was given a new name. His name had been Lucius Domitius Ahenobarbus. Claudius changed the boy's name to Caesar! Caesar Drusus Germanicus." Priscilla paused, then added, "But in Rome he is known by another name."

"And what name is that?"

"In Rome he is called Nero."

"If he succeeds to the throne, what manner of emperor will he be?"

"I can only guess. On one hand we could say he would make a wonderful emperor because Seneca has been his tutor, and Seneca is a good man indeed. On the other hand," continued Priscilla cautiously, "there flows within him the blood of the monster Caligula."

(Priscilla was right in all that she spoke. As long as Seneca was Nero's tutor, he was a much loved and very fair emperor. But Nero later deposed Seneca. After that, with no restraints on him, the madness of Caligula was unleashed in Nero's veins.)

Paul then asked the brother who had come from the docks, "Is there any news that perhaps the Jews might be allowed to return to Rome?"

"No, none."

"It is too soon, is it not?" sighed Paul with resignation. "Perhaps we will have to wait six months or a year. Perhaps longer."

Then Paul added something so quickly that, looking back, it seems he must have been planning it for a very long time.

"Aquila, tonight I wish to dine with you and Priscilla and the eight young men."

That night eight men entered a hushed room. It was Gaius who broke the silence. "We have heard the good news: Claudius is now a god."

Paul responded, bitingly, "It is far better that he be a god than an emperor. Now, brothers, sit down; I have something extremely important about which to talk with you and Priscilla and Aquila."

The only news I, Timothy, ever heard that equaled the news that Paul would go to Ephesus was the news he broke to us that night. It was news that even shook the unshakable Priscilla.

"We have been in Ephesus for just a little over a year," began Paul. "Thanks to the mercies of God and the preparation Priscilla and Aquila made for us by moving to Ephesus before we arrived, it has been easier to work in Ephesus than in any other place I have ever been. Again, I want you to know that we owe so much to Priscilla and Aquila.

"As to the death of Claudius, Rome was in great need of a new god. Of the new emperor, Germanicus Nero, I know nothing. But I will judge the future by the past. The emperor Tiberius once removed all Jews from Rome. As a result, the banking system and the economy of Rome soon began to collapse. It turned out that Hebrews are a little more honest than Italians and much more resistant to bribes and disobeying the laws of Rome. It is my hope that Nero will rescind Claudius's edict. I also hope, with all my heart, that he will back away from some of the burdens that Rome has laid on Israel. If he does not, I see only tragedy ahead."

Paul stared at the floor for a long time. We all knew that something dramatic was about to unfold.

"There are two very important things I have to speak to you about. First, many people have come here from other cities in Asia Minor and have returned to their homes as part of God's redeemed. Many of them have visited the assembly here—some only for a few days, others for weeks or a few for months. With few exceptions, when they have returned to their homes, they have sent word asking that someone come to their city to preach the gospel and raise up a gathering of God's people. It is now time to begin to respond to these requests.

"The hour has come for you brothers to begin going out to these cities. You will have a place to stay wherever you go."

Aristarchus made known all our feelings by releasing an ear-numbing "Hallelujah!"

"You will not all go out at once, neither will you go alone. I will divide you into four pairs. From time to time I will go out with you. Tychicus and Trophimus must go only to observe. They are far, far too young in Christ to carry on the Lord's work. I will have Tychicus go out with Timothy and Trophimus go out with Titus. When I go with you . . . I will not stay as long as you do. I will leave you to the raising up of the body of Christ. But you will always report back to me."

Secundus leaned back until he was flat on the floor. "I think it is time I went home to Greece!"

As expected, Paul ignored this display of humor.

"We will continue in this way until all of you have had the experience of going into a new city, preaching Christ, planting the ecclesia, and also *leaving.*"

This time it was Gaius who let out a "Hallelujah!"

"I hope you brothers will still be this excited after you have been thrown into prison a few times and been well beaten with rods."

Aristarchus rejoined quickly. "I am not a Roman citizen, brother Paul. They will not beat me." Aristarchus paused, then said, "They will crucify me."

"As I said . . . "

"Shall we choose *where* we go," I asked, "or is that your decision?"

"I will choose! Further, Secundus and Aristarchus will not go out together because they are from the same city. Tychicus and Trophimus will not go out together because they are blood brothers and are far too young in the Lord.

"The Lord sent his first disciples out in twos, mark that. But also mark this: Going in twos is neither sacred nor permanent. The ways of God cannot be confined. Today the Twelve do not practice going out in twos. They go wherever the Lord—and sometimes circumstances—lead them. Nor is it true that the person with whom you go out will be the same person with whom you will continue to work. Barnabas and I colabored together across Galatia. But our time together was only *two* years. Silas and I colabored in Greece, but only for two years. I came here to Ephesus without a coworker. Going in twos is good—especially while you are being trained—but it is not sacred. Always remember, your Lord is an untamed lion. He cannot be confined by men's boundaries. In addition, I will not send you far—perhaps no more than fifty or sixty miles from Ephesus.

"One other word. You will preach the gospel, but I cannot promise that it always follows that a church will be raised up. You may be thrown out of the city after only a few days. If so, go to the next city and preach there. Continue until such time as the Lord adds those whom he has chosen to eternal life and who are to assemble.

"Do not feel that you are someone special if the house of God is raised up through your hand. Do not feel that you are a failure if the Lord's house is not raised up. In the Lord's work there is neither success nor failure. And never claim a city as your exclusive territory. You are trainees!

"When you are not traveling," said Paul, emphatically, "you will be a brother in the church. When brothers meet together, you will sit there as just an ordinary believer. I did the same for four years when I first came to Antioch from Troas. Your functioning in the meetings should be no more and no less than that of the other brothers and sisters. You are not special now; you will not be special tomorrow. And you certainly were not special yesterday."

Paul's words were so even and so absolute, we were all a little shaken.

At that moment I said to Paul, "Brother Paul, when we go out to the other cities in Asia Minor, I know where I want to go."

"Already?"

"Yes, definitely!"

"Where?"

"Thyatira."

"Thyatira? Why?"

"First of all, it is because this is where I should go. Second, because it is the home of Lydia."

Paul looked skeptical.

"Timothy, you should never go anywhere to proclaim your Lord on the basis of sentiment. Are you aware that I have never returned to the land of Cilicia to preach the gospel? Never have I raised up the church in my native country. On the other hand, Barnabas wanted very much to return to Cyprus, his homeland.

I felt this was mostly for sentimental reasons, and it was one of the things on which we disagreed. Give it some time and consideration, and talk with me later.

"Now it is time for you brothers to go," said Paul, "for I must talk with Priscilla and Aquila. We will speak together on one of the most important matters the three of us will ever discuss."

As we turned to go, Priscilla spoke. "With words that serious," she said lightly, "I can hardly wait. Please come into the living room, Paul, and let us find out what this momentous hour holds. You are not going to make me go back to the synagogue again, I hope."

"It is nothing so minor," said Paul. "What we are going to discuss may affect an entire nation—and perhaps the world."

Paul's words were prophetic.

"Then speak, and speak well," said Aquila.

CHAPTER 22

Priscilla's eyes were already filled with tears, though Paul had not uttered a word. It was obvious, also, he was completely at a loss as to how to begin.

"How long will it be," he seemed to say to himself, "before any Jew dares set foot back in Rome? Whoever arrives there will be risking his neck."

"You mean, that they will probably get their heads cut off!" said Priscilla with a smile.

"Exactly!" replied Paul. "Oh, the advantages of being a Roman citizen!"

Paul stopped for a moment, then continued his musing. "How long will it be? Not less than a year I am certain. Whenever the empire gets a new Caesar, it seems the entire world waits and watches to see if the new emperor can consolidate his power and thereby secure his throne *and* his power. Yes, at least a year. Who knows . . . it could take five years or even a decade before a Hebrew can safely reenter Rome. One thing is certain," Paul said, turning and looking at Aquila. "Right now you and I are still outlawed from the Imperial City. But when that day does arrive, I want you to seriously consider going back to Rome . . . to be among the *very first* to reenter Rome."

Neither responded. They only waited. Finally, Priscilla

wiped her eyes. "I knew it would be Rome," she said in that precious, unique way that was so much Priscilla. Paul was relieved at the reassuring sparkle in Priscilla's eyes, for Paul knew how serious his request was. He knew, perhaps better than they, that they truly would be risking their very lives if they reentered Rome.

"If you arrive a day too soon," Paul said very slowly and very deliberately, "it *will* cost you your heads!"

"We do not mind risking our necks for Jesus Christ," said Priscilla, speaking with an optimism that seemed to have nothing to do with his statement.

"Aquila, let me make clear to you why I feel you must be among the first of the Jews to return to Rome. As far as we know, there is not a believer left in Rome. All the Christians who once lived there were Jews." Paul's face showed signs of deep concern as he continued, "But Rome is a Gentile city, heathen to the core. The church of Jesus Christ in Rome *must* be a Gentile church. A Gentile city . . . a *Gentile* church. The first believers to enter that city must be Gentiles."

Priscilla nudged Aquila. "Why, that means I will have to go alone, because you, my husband, are a Jew."

"True," said Paul, "but Aquila has lived in a Gentile experience of the ecclesia. For *five* years! That qualifies him to *almost* be a Gentile."

"Then I will let you go with me," said Priscilla teasingly, "but this time you will not drag me into one of those Saturday morning synagogue services! Never!"

"Brother Paul," Aquila responded, answering Paul with all the seriousness with which Paul had spoken, "I was part of only *seven* people who met in the Trastavere district in Rome. It was a Jewish meeting, yes—a Jewish assembly . . . if you could even call it that. Frankly, when we met together, it was more like a dead synagogue meeting. I may be a Jew, but I never want to see anything like those meetings in Rome ever again. My feelings about Rome—and a Gentile church—are as passionate as yours. What I have known in Corinth, what I have experienced here in Ephesus, and what it was like to visit the assemblies in northern Greece—*that* is what I want in Rome. For that I, too, am willing to risk becoming a headless Roman.

"It is absolutely imperative that we be the first ones back into that city. But perhaps it is not as serious a matter as it seems. Already, I understand, Rome is wallowing in fraud. Ever since the Jews left, the city has not been able to find enough honest Gentiles to conduct business without fear of being cheated. Rome is suffering from the lack of the presence of honest Jews. There have already been cries to lift the decree or ignore it.

"Seneca is a wise man. In my judgment, the decree of Claudius will either be lifted or ignored *soon.* If that happens, Hebrews will be pouring back into Rome in great numbers. Frankly, it would be better that the ban be ignored rather than revoked. Hebrews may be a little slower to return than they would if the ban was lifted. That will give the advantage to a Gentile assembly. When the Jewish believers do return—and return they will—they will be returning to discover that the church there is Gentile."

Paul nodded emphatically. "That is the way it *must* be. Not only a Gentile church, but they should encounter a *strong* Gentile church, as strong as any on the face of the earth. Therefore I ask of you, when you do go back—no matter how long that may be—you must *not* settle in the Trastavere district. That district is a Jewish ghetto. You must settle in one of the other thirteen districts of Rome. This *is* possible—because of Priscilla. She is, after all, a Gentile . . . and a Roman! She cannot be forced to live in the Trastavere district."

Aquila turned to Priscilla. "I was so wise to marry a heathen."

"As I have so often told you," responded Priscilla, taking Aquila's hand. She went on to say, "It was three hundred years ago that the first Jews were brought to Rome, and all of them were slaves. About a hundred years ago, by count, there were thirty-five thousand Hebrews in Rome. Over the years most of the Jews have been set free, but even until now they are banished from living on the right side of the Tiber River. In Rome, prejudice runs high against that district. I agree, we must not be in Trastavere. The assembly of God *must* meet north of the Tiber."

Aquila nodded. "It was no one less than Cicero who called us Jews 'barbaric and superstitious.' This attitude still prevails. One reason for these prejudices is that the Jews who live in Rome do not have to pay taxes in Rome. Rather, they are allowed to send their taxes to the Temple in Jerusalem. We are the only people in the world who have such a privilege. This raises deep resentment, especially in times when Rome is experiencing famine or some other hardship. The fact that the Jerusalem Temple is the second largest bank in the world only adds more distrust and envy. We agree, not the Trastavere district."

"Brother Paul," continued Priscilla, "let me remind you what Rome is like. There is no culture that dominates, there is no race that dominates, and there is not even a language that dominates, not even Latin. There is no Rome; there is only a polyglot of a hundred cultures living on seven hills. Is it possible for the church of Jesus Christ, gathering in Rome, to reflect what the city of Rome is?

"That simply means there must be Christians coming to Rome from all over the empire. The believers who live in Rome must also be a polyglot."

"But what of the Jews who have to live in Trastavere? When they return, some among them will be believers, and they will desire to gather with the assembly," said Aquila.

"Then the assembly of Christ must meet very, very near Trastavere . . . just as near as possible."

"There is a solution," said Priscilla. "Aventine Hill. Trastavere is just left of the Aventine district with only the Tiber River between them. A bridge connects the two districts."

"Then it will be the Aventine," responded Paul.

"One more thing. Have I sufficiently impressed upon you what a horrible place Rome is?" inquired Priscilla.

"The bowels of hell cannot be much worse than Rome," agreed Aquila. "People literally die there from lack of sleep. It is the most horrible place on this earth in which to live. People do not live . . . they exist. That city is more noisy and filthy than the human mind can conceive. People walk the streets with flowers pressed to their nose just to endure the stench.

"Brother Paul, try to visualize this: Augustus Caesar divided the city into fourteen *regianes.* Today there are about one million people who live in Rome. While virtually all one million people live in two thirds of the city, yet only thirty-six thousand live in the other third. *They* are the elite. The powerful. The rich. The royal. You might say that one million people in eleven districts serve thirty-six thousand who live in *three.* Most of those million people in eleven districts live under conditions that are simply inhumane."

Priscilla followed up on Aquila's words: "There was a census taken just before we left Rome. Virtually everyone lives—or exists—in places called insulae . . . or apartments. There is only one house for every twenty-six blocks, and the blocks are large. One house for every twenty-six blocks means the rest are *insulae.* People are crammed like cattle into those miserable apartments."

"I can only imagine," said Paul, grimly. "But, yes, I have heard the stories; and, yes, I believe you both."

"No human being should have to live in an insula, and yet almost all of Rome does. Aventine Hill is one place where the noise is almost bearable and the air not too poisoned. It is well centered. It is close to Trastavere. To the north of Aventine Hill is the Roman forum. To the south, Ostian Road, and to the west, the Tiber River. Beyond that, Trastavere. Then to the east, to the right of Aventine Hill, is the Porta Capena district. Trastavere and Porta Capena are the two poorest of the *regianes.* Paul, you can expect that most who become believers will be poor. Most will be slaves or those who have been freed from slavery. I would therefore assume most of our future brothers and sisters will come from those two districts. Fortunately, both districts are near the Aventine."

"Such it has been in all places," agreed Paul. "We are mostly the poor."

"One question, Paul. You are asking two people to go to Rome. There are a million people in that city. Just how do you expect two people to do anything in the way of spreading the gospel?"

"Let us settle another question first," said Paul. "Are you willing to go?"

Priscilla took Aquila's arm and then spoke directly to him. "You found Jesus Christ, and in so doing, so did I. Then we came to Corinth and found the church, our heart's dream! Now we have had the privilege of helping Paul in Ephesus, and we both witnessed what has come from that. Our lives have been a miracle and a joy. Aquila, Paul is no longer young. If ever my people—the heathen—are to know the life of Christ within them, and the life of the ecclesia in the great city of Rome, the best opportunity for this to happen lies with our brother Paul. The door to Rome will be open soon, I am sure. I have no love for Rome, nor do you. But with all my heart I wish to return."

It was Aquila's turn to give his answer. "I am a Jew and very proud of that, but I have found a larger kingdom. Yes, Paul, my wife and I will depart for Rome as soon as that door . . . !" Aquila paused. "As soon as it *appears* we *might* not get our heads chopped off. I do not intend to wait until the door to Rome is fully, clearly open." Aquila choked. "I intend to be there, living in that city in our own house on Aventine Hill before that door opens. It will be a shelter for all the believers in Rome and for those who ever come to Rome." He then added, "Do not misunderstand: Neither of us has any use for that city, but we do for the city of God." Priscilla reached up and gently kissed Aquila on the cheek, her eyes brimming with tears and pride.

Aquila continued forcefully, "We are willing to go. There are many questions, many things to be settled, and much that we do not know! Now, I repeat my question. You do realize that two people are incapable of making any real impression on that city?"

"There are ways," replied a thoughtful Paul. "Later. I will explain *how*, later." There was a confidence in his voice that would have impressed an archangel.

Priscilla stood and addressed her husband: "So many different people and cultures in that vast, insane city. In Corinth, we had to knock down walls in our home to make room for a gathering of the ecclesia. Here in Ephesus we have also knocked down walls. But in the city called Rome we will be breaking down more than mortar and clay. We will be seeking to bring together under one roof entire cultures and languages, as well as political views without number."

Their conversation ended. Aquila's question remained unanswered. No one knew what was on Paul's heart. How could just two believers do anything in a city of a million heathen?

It was not long after this that Paul sat down with Priscilla and Aquila again, as well as with eight young men with them. It was then that Paul told them what was on his heart for Rome. That day came sooner rather than later as Paul came to realize how short his stay in Ephesus would be. And how short a time he probably had to live! The arrival of an unexpected visitor made that point *very* clear.

CHAPTER 23

It was raining. A storm had blown up over Ephesus, but another storm—far greater—was gathering in Corinth. This storm would plunge the ecclesia there into unparalleled crisis. It was an era of crises because yet another storm had broken over Jerusalem and Antioch.

Someone opened the door to Tyrannus's school just as a clap of thunder shook earth and sky. We all turned to see who had brought the roar of thunder into our midst.

"Luke!"

Soaked to the skin, there stood the uncle of Titus, even the beloved physician of Antioch.

Paul rushed over to him. Instantly they began talking in quiet tones. Luke came over to where the eight of us were sitting. We immediately stood and embraced this most respected of men.

"Uncle," said Titus, "it is a long way from Antioch to Ephesus. I assume you are bringing news."

'I am," responded Luke.

"Is it Blastinius?" I asked.

"Not only Blastinius but much more."

Paul motioned for us to sit down again. "I would prefer that Luke and I speak privately. In the meantime, Timothy, make sure that Tychicus and Trophimus hear of our pharisaical friend." Paul's eyes narrowed. "And if you speak of him outside this room, you will never be inside this room again."

"Who is *him?*" asked Tychicus.

Paul dismissed himself and with a drenched Luke headed quickly for the home of Priscilla and Aquila. A little later he sent for Titus, Gaius, and me to join them. (The three of us had met Blastinius face-to-face.)

"What is it?" Titus asked Luke, with no small concern.

"The Daggermen."

"We know," I replied. "Barnabas wrote a letter to Paul about them very recently. We all read the letter. Paul is possibly in danger."

Luke's face darkened.

"Rome is tense. In Israel talk of revolt is everywhere. Almost everyday someone is assassinated. There is now a new secret society in Israel called *the Zealots.*"

"The Zealots?" asked Paul. "That is a strange name to take. When I was young, I was called a zealot, a zealot for the law of Moses. So were others. This term has been with us for centuries."

"But now there is a secret society carrying that name," assured Luke. "Although different from the Daggermen, their end is the same: to strengthen devotion to the law and to throw off the bondage of Rome."

"You have come a long way, brother Luke," said Gaius. "Most of what you have told us we already know. There must certainly be more, or the ecclesia in Antioch would not have sent you."

"The news is simple. After many debates, the Daggermen have decided to mark two more men for death. One is Simon Peter, for they think he has allowed Gentiles, who are uncircumcised, to enter the Temple."

"Tell them the name of the other man," requested Paul, dispassionately.

Luke looked at the three of us, then at Priscilla and Aquila. "The Daggermen have now made a vow to kill Paul. It is a vow to the death. That simply means they will not stop until Paul is dead or until they are dead. The Daggermen are committed to going anywhere in the world to fulfill this vow. *Paul is now a hunted man.*"

"Does that mean," inquired Paul thoughtfully, "that they have already departed Israel and are searching for me?"

"Yes, they have come as far north as Syria looking for you. They thought you were in Antioch. They are not really sure where to go next."

"Interesting," said Paul. "And what of Blastinius?"

Luke could be very engaging, and this was one of his moments. "Brother Paul, you have the gift of upsetting people."

Paul feigned surprise. "I have never heard anyone say such a thing before."

"There is no doubt that at the heart of all of this is Blastinius. He stirs up the brothers and sisters in the ecclesia in Jerusalem. He has a *very* strong following among the believing Pharisees. He stirs up the unbelieving Jews. Yes, and he agitated the Daggermen concerning you. This air of animosity has now spilled over onto the Zealots. But I must add that Blastinius's hate and his vengeance are almost as great toward Peter as they are toward you."

"The assembly in Jerusalem, in general—where do they stand?"

"To my knowledge, there are some who believe you are determined to destroy the law of Moses. That letter you wrote to Galatia is probably the most circulated document in Israel right now."

Paul groaned. "I am surprised. I would think that letter had been forgotten by now, even in Galatia."

"Brother Paul, do not be too surprised. That was quite a

letter you sent us," Gaius commented with a broad smile. "It shook us mightily."

"Blastinius, I am told," said Luke, "still vacillates between being a follower of Christ and one totally consumed with the law of Moses. He is drawing his greater strength from those who oppose any compromise concerning the law."

"Luke, I ask you the question I frequently ask myself: Will Blastinius murder?"

"I doubt it. But he would not hesitate to encourage others to do so."

"Little difference!" mused Paul.

"Would that man dare go back to Galatia?" I asked.

"I think not," responded Luke. "But he may send some believing Pharisees there."

"Do the Galatian churches know this?" asked a distressed Gaius.

"They not only know it, they have completely disregarded the news." A broad grin swept across Paul's face. Gaius shot a fist into the air. I leaned over and grabbed Gaius around the neck.

"Galatia has outgrown the likes of Blastinius!" I added.

"I wholeheartedly agree," said Gaius. "Grace has won over the law. The brothers and sisters in Galatia now know what grace is and what the law is, and they know the difference! They chose grace."

"There is a rumor, and it seems to be true, that Blastinius has sent out two parties of people. One to go to the churches and the other to the synagogues."

"No one has ever come here," said Paul. "Nor Greece."

"For some reason, many think you are in Troas. Paul, do you have friends in Troas?"

For a moment Paul looked confused. "Only a few, and I have paid one very short visit there."

"Well, for some reason, the synagogue in Troas has great

sympathy toward you. A good number of those in the synagogue there have turned to the Lord. On my way here, I was told that a letter came to you in Antioch from Troas. The letter is an invitation for you to come to Troas. Perhaps as many as a hundred people in Troas await your arrival. You did not know?"

"What!" exclaimed Paul. "You do have the gift of bringing good news and bad news at the same time, brother Luke."

"There are rumors that you are also in northern Greece, but I have heard none that you are in Ephesus."

"Perhaps we can start a rumor that I am in Spain," laughed Paul. "Or Britain!"

Paul then asked the most obvious question: "The Daggermen have come only as far as Antioch?"

"Yes, but someday they will find out where you are. Someday, someone is going to come to the synagogue here. Someday, the Daggermen *are* going to find you."

"I am more concerned about Blastinius than the Daggermen," sighed Paul. "It also grieves me to know that he would send Pharisees, who are professing believers, to the churches. It seems Blastinius is reluctant to try to do again in other provinces what he himself did in Galatia. He is sending others in his place. This is *not* good news."

Titus reached over and ruffled my hair. "Perhaps he is afraid that he might once more run into Timothy."

"I do have more to tell you," said Luke. We all groaned.

"Blastinius has not given up his vow and will go to some of the churches. Where he will appear next, I do not know, but one day he *will* discover that you have been in northern Greece. Never doubt . . . Blastinius will go to Greece! While there, he will also discover that you are *not* there!"

Paul dropped his face into his hands. "Greece. Oh, Greece. They will surely receive him with open arms."

At first I thought Paul was acknowledging his pain and his fears. But then I realized that he was once more handing over to his Lord the assemblies in northern Greece. Paul was doing what he did best—he was standing before the Lord and *losing*.

"Paul, he still has the letter from James with him," added Luke.

"Oh no, no, no!" groaned Paul, "I thought better of Blastinius than that."

"Paul, you have warned the churches, have you not, about him? About that letter? You have told them of his coming? Surely by now you have done that, Paul?"

Paul's head snapped up. "Luke, when you left Philippi I said to you, 'Do not tell the believers in Philippi about Blastinius—don't even mention his name.' No Luke, *I have not changed.* They do not know of this man."

Paul looked around the room. "There was a day when Blastinius went to the churches in Galatia. No one expected him—they were unarmed; yet, Blastinius lost. Grace won. Christ triumphed!

"Unwarned, unprepared, unknowing, hospitable in receiving guests in a way that defies explanation. They are innocent—without fear of ghosts."

Then Paul shocked—even dismayed—all of us.

"I look forward to the day that Blastinius is invited into the assemblies to speak, to teach, to try to corrupt, and to attempt to destroy. Even to seek to circumcise. I cannot wait. And when it is all over, then I shall find out if I, Paul of Tarsus, have built with straw or gold."

"We need never fear for the church in Philippi," I said, attempting to introduce a positive air. "First of all, there are virtually no Jews in that city, and there is no synagogue. And there *is* Lydia."

Luke brightened. "Oh yes, there really is Lydia."

"But Thessalonica, that is another matter. I dread the thought of seeing Blastinius come to that city and stir up the synagogue once more," said Paul, grimacing.

"*And* the local government," I added.

"I have laid a foundation, and his name is Christ. I must believe that Thessalonica will survive. The ecclesia is God's building; Blastinius is the fire. No matter what work any man does, some day—some way—a man's work will be tried by fire. Fire *must* come. Always! Fire must come!

"You all know that while I was walking from Philippi to Thessalonica, the Lord showed me why he had put this man in my life. God took my strength away and gave me weakness in its place. God then honored me by placing Blastinius in my life. Consequently, every day I live, I must ask myself this question: Paul of Tarsus, are you building with gold, silver, and costly stone, or with straw? For this . . . this thorn from God; I thank him that Blastinius is in my life. All men tend toward legalism. There is only one cure for legalism. Sometimes fire must burn out that legalism before the cure is fully known."

I knew exactly what Paul was referring to when he referred to *only one cure* for legalism—so did Titus. But Luke did not.

"And what is that cure?" asked the beloved physician.

"His name is Jesus Christ. His name is freedom." Paul's voice resonated with conviction.

"As long as man is on this earth, there will be legalists, there will be rule makers, there will be men whose minds are filled with the word *do* and the word *don't.* Those legalists will always despise the gospel of grace. A revelation of Christ and Christ alone will banish such legalistic tendencies from our soul."

"Paul," said Gaius, "someday the believers in the churches are going to ask you why you did not warn them about

Blastinius. What on earth will you say to them? Have you a *sane* defense?"

"That is simple. I will tell them I was too busy proclaiming Jesus Christ."

We all cheered!

Paul then said something that was both painful and precious. "It is better that I not build at all if I cannot build with Christ alone. It is better that I not be one sent by God to raise up the bride of Christ if, when the fire falls, the work is consumed."

"It really is true what they say about you, Paul," observed Luke.

"What is that?" asked Gaius.

Luke looked at Gaius and shook his head. "You do not know? Surely you *do* know. Some say he is mad."

Paul broke in, "Then let this madman speak.

"I am no better than Blastinius with his 620 *do's* and *don'ts* of the law . . . no better than he, if, when I preach, I have no better weapons at my disposal than the weapon of *fear!* I will not warn, and I will not cause his children to fear. The foundation I build on is Christ, the material is Christ, the cornerstone is Christ."

Paul then spat out his next words: "And let the devil have everything else!"

We were all stunned. Luke blinked. It was very rare to see Paul angry.

In that moment of heavy silence, Paul spoke slowly, adding, "I do not believe Blastinius can succeed. And if he sends his cohorts, I believe . . . *they* . . . shall . . . fail."

We talked for only a few more minutes. After that, we were on our faces before our Lord.

Paul did not know that his life was about to be thrust into yet another great crisis, a period of darkness, distress, and despair. Only once before, when Paul traveled the road from Philippi to Thessalonica, was it ever so dark.

Paul had just heard grave news about forces from without working against him and against the church. In a few days he would be receiving news of forces from *within* a church, forces that were about to rip a church completely apart. If he were here today, Paul would tell you that he would gladly face enemies from without a thousand times over those that come from within.

Alas, Paul was about to hear of the disaster taking place in Corinth.

More than anyone else, other than Paul, Titus would become embroiled in that sad affair. It is, therefore, left to me, Timothy, to tell you of the dreadful hour that Paul was destined to pass through and the role that my dearest friend, Titus, played in this high drama.

CHAPTER 24

"Titus! Timothy!"

I recognized the voice immediately.

It was the slave (and brother) Sebastian, who belonged to the household of Chloe and who on an earlier journey to Ephesus had informed Paul of Peter's impending visit to Corinth. Sebastian was usually accompanied by Aelius and Zoninius, brothers who were often with Sebastian on his travels from Corinth to Ephesus.

"Back again in Ephesus? The House of Chloe must be doing a great deal of business in Asia Minor," said Titus. "How is the gathering in Corinth?"

"Corinth is the busiest city in the empire. As to the church, is Paul presently here in Ephesus?"

"Yes, and he will surely want to hear from you," I responded.

"I must make my visit brief for I am only here until dawn. My ship sails for Corinth at that time. But I must see Paul. Please take me to him." There was anxiety in Sebastian's voice.

We rushed about everywhere trying to find Paul. It was late evening before we succeeded. (Paul was just arriving at the home of Priscilla.) Within a moment, we were deep in conversation.

"First," said Sebastian, "the church in Corinth has sent the brothers Stephanas, Fortunatus, and Achaicus to Ephesus to speak with you, Paul. They sailed *before* I did, but my ship arrived here first. The ship they took stops *everywhere*, whereas the one I sailed on came directly to Ephesus. The situation in Corinth is not good. Strangely enough, when these three brothers arrive, they will know less about the situation in Corinth than I do. On the other hand, their news may be more accurate than mine. What I know is what I learned just before sailing. Please remember that even firsthand news is not always accurate, so I can only imagine how correct my secondhand information is. The last time I was here, I told you of Peter's visit to Corinth. Do you know that Apollos came to Corinth soon afterward?"

"No," replied Paul. "Is Apollos still in Corinth?"

"No, Peter sailed from Corinth to North Africa, and Apollos is somewhere else in Greece, but he is not in Corinth."

Sebastian looked straight at Paul. "Brother, the news is not good. There is a deep fracture in the Corinthian assembly. Emotions and opinions are running *very* high."

Paul felt he had already heard all the bad news he could handle, from Luke. Distraught, he knew that what he was about to hear might be more than he could bear. Paul laid his head in his hands. "Continue," he said.

"While Apollos was with the assembly, a great deal of criticism about him developed. The criticism came from the Jews in the church. Paul, I must be honest."

Paul waved his hand.

"The difference between Peter and Apollos is great—Peter being the more careful. On the other hand, there are those in the gathering who are enthralled by Apollos. A few have publicly said, 'Apollos is greater than Peter or Paul.'"

Paul looked up; his mouth dropped.

"The Jews are very offended at that statement. The Jewish believers in the gathering are extremely unhappy about *all* this talk of Apollos. In my judgment this may have a great deal to do with the difference between Jews and . . . well . . . us heathen. As for me, being a barbarian slave from the far, far north, I hardly understand what the problem is. All I know is that the Jews fell in love with Peter, and the Greeks are very taken with Apollos.

"Others in the church are trying to reconcile the two groups. They keep reminding everyone that it was you, Paul, who planted the church in Corinth. This has only caused more tension."

Sebastian shook his head sadly. "And then there are those who say, 'We don't need Peter, we don't need Paul, we don't need Apollos—all we need is Jesus.' "

Paul grimaced."Oh . . . ! Oh . . . !"

Both Titus and I understood that the greatest danger lay with the attitude of the fourth group. We had been in the life and experience of the ecclesia a long time and recognized that the dreamers and the theorists had an ethereal view of the church (and everything else that has to do with spiritual matters). No church survives unless it has outside help.

Paul began asking questions. Sebastian, as always, responded well. The longer the conversation went on, the grimmer we all became. I, Timothy, well remember my own thoughts: *No ecclesia has ever been in a situation like this. Corinth may be headed for disintegration. Can even Paul find a solution to all these tangles?*

When believers turn against the one who planted the church, it is a time of crisis like no other. There is little hope for a saving solution.

"Just how deep do these fissures go?" asked Paul. "Have the brothers and sisters actually built walls between one another?"

"I do not know. Perhaps when Stephanas, Fortunatus, and

Achaicus arrive from Corinth—they should arrive soon—they will be able to give you clearer answers. Nonetheless, Paul, there is something I know those three brothers do not know. It has to do with something that took place after Stephanas left."

"And that is?"

"I am ashamed to tell you," replied Sebastian.

You could almost see Paul's heart breaking. "I am an old man," said Paul. "I do not think I will be *too* surprised."

"I am not so sure, Paul," stammered Sebastian. "One of the brothers in the church has begun living with his father's wife."

Paul's face whitened.

"Wha . . . ?"

"We have all seen this coming for some time. In fact, it has probably been going on for quite some time, but now it is in the open; the man *is* living with her . . . with his father's wife!"

"That is considered immoral!"

"Yes," replied Sebastian sadly.

"Why have not the brothers in the ecclesia taken some kind of action?"

Sebastian shrugged his shoulders. "I have no idea."

At that moment I knew beyond all doubt that Corinth was about to receive a letter from Paul of Tarsus. A very *strong* letter.

Paul was a man of great patience, and that includes being understanding in a world that is *a*moral. However, for the church to sanction—that is, to be passive—in the presence of such extreme immorality right there *in* the body of Christ was more than *even Paul* could abide.

"There has previously been immorality in the ecclesia. I suppose there always will be. But there has never been anything so evil. And *never* has an assembly sat by, doing nothing!"

"I must leave," interrupted Sebastian. "My ship. It is necessary I be on the ship before it sails. And it sails at dawn."

"Thank you for coming, Sebastian. I am your debtor."

Sebastian paused at the door. "If you write to Corinth, will you please tell them a servant of the House of Chloe was the one who told you these things? But I also ask that you let them know that I was not certain of everything that I have said to you. Now, is there anything that you want me to deliver in the way of a message to Corinth?"

"Tell them that the assembly in Ephesus is growing and is strong. Tell them that the eight young brothers whom I am training are giving me only a few problems. And tell them I am considering writing them a letter."

"Paul," said Titus, "would you like to mention to them that the crowds listening to you in the marketplace are growing? Also, I am sure that many—the Jews in particular—might like to know what is happening to your headbands . . . the Jews *love* miracles."

I, Timothy, had no idea what Titus was talking about and said so.

"The sweatbands that Paul puts around his head everyday when he leaves Tyrannus's house and goes back to work in the marketplace—they disappear. He has to put on a new one every day. The mystery is this: The headbands are worthless rags."

"Why, Paul?" I asked.

"Souvenirs? I suppose it is souvenirs. This town is given to such things."

"Timothy, it is more than that," Titus contended. "Rumor has it that Paul's headbands *heal.* I thought Corinth would enjoy hearing that—at least the Jews might."

"Sebastian, please do *not* take that rumor to Corinth," growled Paul.

Sebastian nodded and with that bade us good-bye. Then he remembered something else.

"Oh, I forgot," said Sebastian, reentering the house. "Do

you remember that list of questions we Corinthians drew up for you last year?"

"It is not a thing easily forgotten, brother Sebastian."

"Well, the ecclesia in Corinth is sending you yet another list of questions."

Paul groaned.

"Fortunatus is bringing the list."

"Thank you," said Paul, struggling not to show his consternation.

After Sebastian departed, Paul sighed and said, "Oh my dear, dear Corinthians! Here you are on the verge of disintegrating. Further, there is immorality among you . . . yet in the midst of all that, you send me yet another list of questions!

"I pray to God that Fortunatus's ship arrives soon. We are running out of time. The church in Corinth could splinter at any moment."

Paul got his wish. The ship arrived shortly thereafter. But, as Sebastian predicted, the news Fortunatus brought was grave.

CHAPTER 25

It was a quiet, moonlit evening that brought the ship bearing Stephanas and his two companions from Corinth. After spending the night aboard ship, Stephanas, Achaicus, and Fortunatus made their way into Ephesus.

Aquila greeted them at the door, settled them in, and hurried to the market to find Paul. Paul immediately abandoned his work and rushed toward Priscilla's home. After an exchange of warm greetings, the conversation went straight to the matter of the crisis in the church in Corinth.

"Tell me everything, but first, you need to know that Sebastian was here just two days ago. He departed Corinth after you did, but because he boarded a ship headed straight for Ephesus, he arrived here before you. Several things that he told me are things you do not know about. They occurred *after* you left Corinth."

Because Titus and I lived in the home of Aquila, we wanted very much to know what was being discussed.

Later in the night Paul knocked on the door to our room.

"Timothy, I am seriously considering writing a letter to Corinth, but there is so much to remember; please find pen and parchment and come. I want you to make a few notes."

Leaving the room, I felt I was abandoning Titus. I reminded Paul of this. A few minutes later I stuck my head back into our room and said, "Titus, unworthy heathen, I have interceded for you, dear infidel, come . . . "

Titus threw a sandal at me.

When we went into Paul's room, we found him sitting on the floor, his face flushed and swollen. Seeing us, he struggled to regain his composure but found it hard to breathe, much less speak. His whole body was shaking. He looked up at us and managed to say, "It is as bad in Corinth as I had feared. No! It is worse.

"Timothy, please take notes of what these men say. But first, I must tell you that these brothers were not certain of immorality in the ecclesia. It seems, if it is true, the son began living with his father's wife *after* they departed Corinth."

"Perhaps we saw this coming, but we were not sure," confessed Stephanas. "Besides, we find it very difficult to meddle in someone else's life. When should the church intervene?"

"We do not always know," Paul replied. "This is an ongoing problem in all the assemblies." Turning to us, he continued. "Nonetheless, I have said to these brothers that, though it is very difficult to know what to do even when all the facts are present, the assembly should have done *something*. The one place to draw the line is when there is open sexual immorality *in* the church.

"We are tolerant of everything and patient with everyone. Nonetheless, open, flaunted sexual immorality that is not repented of must never be condoned in the body of Christ. Left alone, such a thing will destroy the ecclesia."

The most tolerant, nonlegalistic man whom I, Timothy, ever knew was speaking of the one matter with which he had no patience: open immorality, unaddressed.

"My three Corinthian brothers have just said to me: 'Jews

have a *custom* of sexual fidelity, whereas Greeks do not. Therefore, the Greeks have a difficult time grasping *purity*.'"

Paul's brow furrowed. "Brothers, this kind of immorality is not a matter of custom. Sexual immorality in the church is not, and will not, be tolerated. Even the world does not condone this!"

I was trying furiously to write down the essence of Paul's words. At the same time I was learning a great deal. So was Titus.

"A believer may do reprehensible things . . . but these do not separate him from God's grace . . . and God's love . . . but . . . " Paul paused. "But, for a testimony to men and angels, there are things that ought not be allowed to continue—not *in* the ecclesia." He took a deep breath and then another.

At that point Paul held up a parchment. "I have a long list of questions these brothers have brought me from the Corinthian believers. I find it a little difficult to see myself answering them in the midst of so grave a crisis. Oh, the Greeks! Sons of Socrates!"

Paul unrolled the scroll.

"Asking questions while the world is falling apart around them."

Paul looked at the list of questions, trying hard to shift his thoughts to such lesser issues.

"Timothy, do you remember how many lawsuits there were in Corinth over buying, selling, and trading?"

I nodded.

"Well . . . it seems two brothers are suing one another as a result of a trade they *thought* they had made. They are going to trial!"

Titus sat straight up. I covered my face.

"The heathen will hear of this! Two brothers in Christ,

fighting with one another *publicly!*" Paul dropped his head in grief.

"Does this mean that there is no one in the assembly wise enough to settle this dispute?" Paul's eyes glistened with hot tears. "Make note of this, would you, Timothy? And, Stephanas, make sure that I state this accurately.

"Am I correct in my understanding of this next question: There are two brothers who, until recently, were friends? One is a meat eater; the other is a vegetarian? Then one day in the marketplace, the vegetarian saw his meat-eating friend go into Lucius's butcher shop." Paul turned to me, "Timothy, you know this shop?"

I looked over at Titus. "It is the largest butcher shop in Corinth."

Paul continued, "The meat-eating brother brought out a very large piece of meat. A moment later the vegetarian rushed into Lucius's shop and asked, 'The man who just left—did he buy meat that had been offered to idols?'

"Lucius answered gruffly, 'Of course he did. Most of the meat in this shop was offered to idols. There are so many people coming to this city to make offerings to the great goddess Aphrodite that there is more meat left in the temple than the priests know what to do with. So the priests sell the meat to me. *Cheap!* And I sell it *cheap*. These offerings support the temple, and the meat offered there supports *me*.'

"The vegetarian brother was devastated. Now the whole assembly is divided over the matter. Oh, Corinth . . . oh dear, dear Corinth!

"So, we have a crisis about sexual immorality, questions about lawsuits, and a falling-out over people's eating habits. Have the brothers and sisters nothing better to cause divisions? Stephanas, there is a deeper issue here—it is the matter of one man laying down his life for another."

"But which man?" replied Fortunatus. Everyone laughed. But Paul was quick with a sobering answer.

"The *stronger* one! The strong one *always* lays down his life for the weaker. And if he cannot do that, then I question whether he is the stronger. Perhaps he is only drawing his strength from the will of his flesh."

All this time I was writing as fast as my hand could move.

"Now, let us see, was there anything else I wanted you to make note of?

"Yes! Write down a sentence about the way the brothers and sisters in Corinth took the Lord's Supper together one particular evening." Then Paul added sardonically: "That must have been one incredible dinner!" He went on to explain.

"While those in the ecclesia were eating together, in the midst of the meal, they took the Lord's Supper. For some reason, on that occasion, they had decided that each person would bring his own food. As you know, there are many brothers and sisters in that assembly—and in all the assemblies—who have virtually no food at all. Others are quite well-to-do. Some sat there, hungry. Others overate . . . and . . . in the course of the meal, several got *drunk!*"

I dropped my pen. Titus choked. The three brothers from Corinth bowed their heads in justifiable shame.

(Paul was both hurt and angry. It can be said, to his honor, that after a few days of dealing with his feelings, Paul would emerge with both understanding and compassion for the Corinthians. The Paul whom I knew understood the frailty of man. In moments of anger, he always waited. When he *eventually* resurfaced, he came forth with forbearance, understanding, and a limitless practice of grace. Nonetheless, over this particular issue, he went through several days of intolerance before he found his way back to grace.)

For several minutes Paul just sat there. At first, I thought it had to do with the drunkenness. But no, it was about something Titus and I had not yet heard about. It was the *internal* crisis—a crisis in the church greater than anything Paul had ever faced.

"*Peter!*" said Paul, slowly. "*Apollos!*" Paul began to sob.

"Corinth is on the verge of catastrophe. I have dreamed . . . I have hoped . . . I have longed for the day when Peter would come to Corinth. From all I have heard, Peter's time there was wonderful. There was great healing . . . glorious meetings. Many came to believe in Christ. Many were healed in the market-place.

"The *Jews* in the assembly were in absolute *bliss.*

"Peter had to leave much sooner than anyone had wanted. When he departed, I am told that hundreds made their way to the ship to see him off."

Paul forced a smile. "Then, shortly thereafter, Apollos came back to Corinth. He was there for quite a long time—his power to speak was at its greatest—and while Apollos was speaking with his incredible oratorical skills, the *Greeks* in the assembly were in absolute *bliss.*"

Stephanas broke in. "I am a Greek, and I have to say that the general impression of those who have a Greek culture would argue that Apollos brought the greatest messages any Greek has ever heard. His voice roared like thunder and then dropped to a whisper. He quoted the ancient philosophers and the greatest of our poetry and told stories of ancient Greek wars. At the same time, he always weaved his words together to make his point as it applied to the gospel. He brought every Greek in the room to tears—or to their feet. By that, I mean that when Apollos finished speaking, all the Greeks in the room jumped to their feet and began applauding wildly.

"Apollos also spoke in the agora. Large crowds came to hear him there. Nonetheless, the truth is, most of those hearing him in the market seemed more interested in his oratorical skills than in the message itself. By the way, Apollos's favorite place to speak is in the *propylaea.*"

(Stephanas explained to Gaius that the propylaea is the broad stairway in Corinth that leads up to the marketplace.)

Fortunatus took the conversation from there. "Apollos departed from Corinth recently. But . . . since he left, the church has moved into four different camps. The Jews want an ecclesia that emphasizes miracles, signs, and wonders—a reflection of Peter's ministry. The Greeks want an ecclesia in which there is a greater emphasis on messages—actually on oratorical skills. The Greeks want to introduce the traditional heathen trappings that go with the Greek sermon: quoting from great philosophers, reciting poems, retelling great episodes in history, and—in general—following Aristotle's way of orations, speech making, and rhetoric."

"Shades of Aristotle," replied a shocked Titus.

"In other words, one group enjoys *seeing;* the other enjoys *hearing,*" observed Paul.

Fortunatus continued, "Whenever Apollos finishes speaking, we Greeks feel we have learned a great deal of *wisdom.*"

"Sophia!" muttered Paul.

"What is sophia?" Titus whispered.

"Wisdom," I replied. "*Greek* wisdom."

"On the other hand," enjoined Stephanas, "the Jews feel refreshed when they see a healing or a sign."

Fortunatus added, "One brother summed it up this way: 'Some think God is with Peter; some think God is with Apollos.' "

I bled for Paul.

We sat; we waited.

Finally, Paul spoke.

"The assembly in Corinth reflects little of an understanding of the Lord Jesus Christ. It is not what a Jewish *eye* sees. It is not what the Greek's *ear* hears. It is not what a man can *imagine.* Neither the miracle, which satisfies the eye, nor the sermon, which satisfies the ear, nor the imaginations of men . . . *none* of these have anything to do with Jesus Christ."

There was pain evident on Paul's face. And a bit of the same on all our faces. "Do not underestimate your problem, my brothers. I have been told that there are those saying, 'Who is Paul? For Paul never worked as many miracles as Peter.' Others are saying, 'Paul never gave us the wisdom that Apollos has given us. Further, Paul is a very poor speaker. Worse, he speaks very poor Greek.' "

Paul's next words stunned all of us.

"Are there those who wish me not to return?" asked Paul.

I, Timothy, was speechless.

"I suppose there is that possibility," said Fortunatus soberly.

Now it was Titus who was struggling to breathe.

"When we were leaving Corinth, a brother said to me at the dock, 'We have many problems in Corinth, but I really doubt that Paul has the ability, or courage, to deal with the situation here. His letters are heavy, but when he is among us, he is a very weak man. A weak man cannot solve our problems.' "

"Then that fellow does not know the Paul I know!" Titus blurted angrily.

"Nor the Paul I know," I agreed. "Perhaps I should tell you, brothers, what it was like to see Paul stoned in Lystra . . . and you might be interested in hearing what I saw when Paul faced the magistrates in Philippi—they wilted under his wrath!"

"And I can tell you of a Paul who, with his considerable nose, faced down Peter. Further, he held out alone before even the *Twelve!*" continued Titus. "Paul is the kindest and most patient man I know—and, yes, he is weak. But there is a strength in his weakness that few people are aware of."

Paul motioned for both of us to be silent.

"Timothy," he said gruffly, "are you writing notes to help me remember, or are you here just to tell stories? Titus, how do you think the Twelve would feel if they heard what you just said?"

"See," I exclaimed.

Ignoring me completely, Paul spoke again: "Perhaps the man who spoke to you at the dock in Corinth was right, Fortunatus. Perhaps I will never be able to return to Corinth. And if I do return, I may not be able to resolve this crisis.

"Here is my conclusion: On the basis of all I have heard today, I have decided it is imperative that I write a letter to Corinth. But I fear that, when it is read, truly . . . they may never want me back again.

"I will give much consideration to the writing of this letter, even to the answering of that endless list of questions! But now, it is time for our three travelers to rest. Fortunatus, before you retire, please give me that list of questions. I will continue to look it over and see if the Lord can give me a word as to how to respond. As to these other matters—the serious ones—I must wait on the Lord for wisdom, which I simply do not possess.

"Fortunatus, brother Stephanas, brother Achaicus, please make yourselves at home here in Ephesus. We invite you to all the meetings. Be aware that the assembly in Ephesus is not the assembly in Corinth; each assembly is, of course, different from all the others. I believe you will enjoy Ephesian hospitality immensely. And please feel free to join us in the afternoon at the school of Tyrannus. We meet there every day. At this particular time, Luke, of Antioch, is with us. Come and join us there."

Paul then added, "I will probably call all of you together again in a few days . . . after I find what it is I should say in a letter."

Unknowingly, Paul had acted wisely in putting off, until later, another such meeting. The very next day Paul did something in the marketplace that eventually stirred up the entire city.

Join me now, in the marketplace, with a man named Sceva and his seven sons.

CHAPTER 26

"This *power* has something to do with the name *Jesus,*" whispered Sceva to his many sons.

For days eight Jewish magicians had been watching Paul in the marketplace, seeking to understand exactly what incantation Paul used to heal the sick and to cast out spirits. There was also the mystery of Paul's headbands that interested them. But mostly it was Paul's "incantation" that intrigued them.

"As best as I can tell, he lays a hand on them and then says, 'In the name of Jesus . . . ' "

The day after our meeting with Stephanus, Paul was back in the marketplace quietly working on the reparation of a tent. He looked up when he saw some people bringing a demon-possessed wretch to him. Paul cast out the spirit. Perverse minds, watching with perverse eyes, decided that they now knew exactly from whence Paul's power came. As foolish as foolish men can be, they decided to try that same *power* to achieve this same end . . . for gain.

Sceva could hardly wait to find someone who was demon possessed. When he did, Sceva said to the demon, "I command you by Jesus, whom Paul preaches, to come out!"

From deep within the possessed man came these haunting words: "I know Jesus, and I know Paul. But who are you?"

At that, the possessed man, suddenly filled with superhuman strength, attacked one son of Sceva after another, ripping off their clothes and beating them brutally.

The sons fled in terror, naked and badly injured. There were few in the marketplace who did not witness at least some part of this event. Some were terrified, while others stood in mystified awe.

As the story passed through the city, people gave new heed to Paul's words. Consequently, over the next few days, there came to the ecclesia an ingathering of new believers.

To understand what happened next, you must know more about the citizens of Ephesus and the way they think.

Ephesus is a city *obsessed* with magic. If you should walk through the city streets, you will see magicians and sorcerers everywhere. Could such a sordid fact fall out to advance the gospel? In this case, it did.

Among other things, the Ephesian citizens believe they can cast spells on their enemies. They also believe in curses. There are magicians and sorcerers aplenty to sell these spells and curses or whatever one may want. The magicians sell *abracadabras*, which are nothing more than strips of parchment. The buyer places them on some part of his body, hoping they will cure an ache or pain or disease.

One of the reasons men and women come from all over the world to Ephesus is to study the occult. They come to learn the powers of darkness. The mediums, in turn, advertise their charms to the new arrivals by means of pantomime and dances. Their dances are accompanied by weird, discordant music, all aimed at luring prospective buyers. The emperor himself maintains a personal astrologer in Ephesus!

(I, Timothy, have stood in the streets of Ephesus and watched these soothsayers and purveyors of chance selling cures and curses in assortments of thousands. But without your seeing it, this scene is impossible to describe.)

That is why Paul's sweatbands were disappearing! Many in Ephesus had seen Paul sitting in the market mending tents and laying his hands on some of the brothers and sisters who, in turn, were often healed. To these superstitious onlookers the sweatband on Paul's forehead was an *abracadabra.*

There sat a man in the middle of all this dark heathenism who mended tents and who never once thought of using the power of God for gain. Therefore, those who were driven by superstition concluded, "If he will not sell it, we will steal it."

It is the temple of Artemis (in Latin, *Diana*) that set this tone for the entire city. There are stories of healing powers coming from Artemis's temple, which is but one more reason people come to Ephesus from all over the empire: They come hoping to be healed as they worship Artemis-Diana.

Diana's temple is situated on a high hill overlooking the city. After climbing the hill, you arrive at the foot of the temple and then ascend fourteen steps. These steps surround the temple on all sides. The temple itself is 377 feet long and 180 feet wide. At the time I, Timothy, lived in Ephesus, this temple was the largest single building in the world. (Nero's home has since surpassed it in size.)

The roof of the temple is supported by columns sixty feet high. There are 170 columns, each six feet wide. These fluted pillars, in double rows, hold up the temple. Everything about the temple is made of marble except the pillars in the inner chamber, which are made of green jasper. In the center of the temple is a vast purple curtain, and behind that the idol Artemis. Rumor has it that the idol is really nothing more than a blackened piece of ancient wood.

It is *this* temple that breeds the superstitions that abound in Ephesus. As a result, wherever you turn there are men selling small replicas of Diana and her temple. Such trinkets are made of silver, a few are made of gold, while most are made of brass.

These tiny replicas of the temple are looked upon as good-luck charms. Virtually every house in Ephesus has at least one. Replicas of Diana, with her three crowns upon her head, are perhaps the largest single source of income for the city. Tens of thousands of visitors coming to Ephesus every year have made the temple in Ephesus the third-largest bank in the world, with only the bank in Rome and the Temple in Jerusalem larger.

(Miniatures of the temple and of the statue of the goddess made so much money that the city, when threatened by a perceived competitor, unleashed its wrath on Paul.)

With all this is mind, you will understand why the attention of the citizens of Ephesus was drawn to a man in the city named Paul, who had great power—as Sceva's sons had proven.

It is hard to believe, but it is true, that in the next two days virtually every one of the 250,000 people who lived in Ephesus had heard the story of Sceva and his sons. That one word, *Jesus*, spread through the city like fire.

Nor was our brother Paul about to pass up this moment of opportunity to declare Jesus Christ in the market. Hundreds listened. Some wondered, some asked questions (mostly about magic, demons, and charms), and many believed.

Somehow or other, when Paul was asked a question, he always managed to turn the inquiry so that it had but one answer—*Jesus Christ.*

"I thought we had seen marvelous things in Corinth," Paul remarked one evening in a meeting of the assembly, "but I have never witnessed so many people believing in the Lord as here."

But when anyone in the market asked Paul about magic, he also denounced it. And then he denounced all the magicians in the city. "They are frauds," he declared. Paul's words came to receptive ears, for deep in their hearts almost everyone in the city already knew that. Nonetheless, they managed both to see the magicians as frauds and at the same time depend on them.

Paul gathered the new believers and told them in no uncertain words that they must renounce their use of magic and incantations. "This must be a part of the proof of your repentance toward God. Nor ought you to be baptized in Jesus' name without the end of such practices."

In the meetings Paul made note that there were *magicians* among the converts. He made it very clear to them that they must give up their trickery. The Holy Spirit seared Paul's words into the hearts of all who heard.

Some of these ex-magicians had become very devout in their faith in Jesus Christ. Consequently, a number of magicians-turned-believers met together, came to an agreement, then marched into the market and publicly denounced the foolishness of charms. These men even confessed their own deceptions to the watching crowd. They went even further. They revealed the secrets of the other magicians. It was not long before the soothsayers and workers of magic found themselves, if not out of a job, at least not as busy as they had been. In the weeks that followed, the magicians' guild fell on hard times.

One former soothsayer announced in the market that he would publicly burn his books of magic on the following day. He then invited all of the other believers to come and watch. He challenged the other ex-magicians to do likewise. This audacious announcement caught the attention of the entire city.

The next day the market was jammed with onlookers. This bold brother lit a fire and began throwing his books into it. Some of the newly converted followers of Jesus began to throw their idols and their bronze statues of the temple of Artemis into the fire. The crowd gasped as more ex-magicians joined in, throwing their potions, their charms, and other dark objects into the fire. Other new believers—and other magicians convicted by what they saw—ran to their homes, seized their charms, idols, good-luck pieces, and books of magic, and rushed back to the market, ending their evil deeds in fire. Book after book was thrown into the blaze. The parchment burned quickly, thereby making a large, bright, and very hot flame. Others, caught up in the moment, who had never even heard Paul speak, began throwing their idols and abracadabras on the fire.

I, Timothy, witnessed this scene. There were several moments when it appeared the entire city was going to forsake its evil practices. But even then, I observed that many of the merchants were looking on in horror. They had every reason to do so. It was estimated that the value of the books burned that day was the equivalent of fifty thousand days of pay—that is, 50,000 denarii.

When the fire burned low, Paul took his place in front of the embers and proclaimed the gospel of Jesus Christ. He did so with a fire greater than the one we had just witnessed.

Titus and I stood, arm in arm, hardly believing what our eyes saw. What we did not foresee was that the story of this day was going to spread all over Asia Minor.

From this one incident many doors opened to us in areas throughout the province. The story of the burning reached down to the city of Magnesia, which is south of Ephesus, and many there came to hear Paul preach. The same happened in Colophon, a city northwest of Ephesus. Others came from Smyrna, which is thirty miles to the north. Citizens of Sardis (thirty miles to the northeast) also came. There were yet others who came from Pergamum, and yes, to my delight, a good number of people from Thyatira (Lydia's hometown), who walked some sixty miles just to hear Paul.

Beyond our wildest dreams, Ephesus had become a sounding board for the gospel to that entire area.

We, the eight, had previously preached in some of those

cities from which people had traveled to Ephesus, had heard Paul, and had believed. When these new believers returned to their hometowns, they began to assemble or write to us and ask us to come and help them.

Suddenly we were hearing from places that we had never heard of and where we had never preached. We were deluged with invitations to come to these cities and raise up the ecclesia.

(Almost everyone who received the Lord during this season remained in Ephesus long enough to be in at least one or two meetings. Attending meetings quickly made new converts want the ecclesia in their city.)

As a result, eight young men were soon speaking in the marketplaces of many nearby cities. We were being given an opportunity beyond even Paul's hopes to proclaim Christ as Savior to unbelievers. We were the most joyful, exuberant young men in the entire world. And the church was planted throughout Asia Minor.

The Ephesian assembly was a place of unbridled joy. Meetings were held every morning and evening. The meetings in Priscilla's home lasted longer and longer as more and more new believers stood to tell the incredible story of how they came to encounter Jesus Christ. Tears, shouts of joy, and late-night endings marked every meeting.

Paul was especially thrilled to learn that both Jews and Gentiles had come all the way from Troas to hear him speak. An assembling of God's people soon arose effortlessly in that ancient city of the Trojans.

(Oddly, Paul was held in great esteem in the Troas synagogue. Despite all that Blastinius had done and all he would later attempt to do, the gospel was destined to prevail in Troas.)

I must confess that the people who received our quickest attention were those who came from Colosse. It was out of our love and respect for Epaphras that we gave extra care to speak to these people and to tell them about Epaphras and Philemon, and to make sure they knew, when they returned home, exactly how to find Philemon's house. The two neighboring towns, Hierapolis and Laodicea, also received our special attention.

If you should ever pass through Asia Minor, you will discover virtually every town and city near the coast—and many towns in the interior—have a witness for the Lord and for his bride. The reason is clear. Within ten years after Paul cast out that demon, there were more assemblies in the little province of Asia Minor than any other place on earth except Israel.

Unfortunately, Achaicus, Stephanas, and Fortunatus did not witness most of the events just recorded. Of necessity they had to return to Corinth only a few days after the sons of Sceva's disastrous encounter with the demon. But they saw enough to know that signs, wonders, miracles, and healings were not the exclusive property of Peter. Watching Paul preach in the marketplace, though his use of the Greek language was rough, they witnessed an anointing upon Paul that Apollos simply did not have.

But please remember, in the midst of these joyful days, Paul was facing Blastinius's continued determination to destroy him, the heartbreaking troubles in Corinth, and the possibility of being assassinated by Daggermen. (One day all these events came together, along with the later disappearance of Titus, plunging Paul into such hopelessness that would cause him to one day cry out, "I despaired of life.")

Paul, Titus, and I sat down with Fortunatus, Stephanas, and Achaicus and read aloud the questions the Corinthians had asked Paul to answer. I can still see Paul's face as he struggled with the grim realities unfolding in Corinth. I watched the pain as he struggled to find answers. His agony was born primarily of fear that the church in Corinth might disintegrate.

Should you ever read the letter Paul wrote to Corinth, remember as you do, that Paul hid his central fear—the fear that he might never see the believers in Corinth again. He knew that the church might well annihilate itself over petty differences. His pain is there in every line. I know, I was present at the writing of that letter.

I, Timothy, will now tell you of the very day the letter was written. But first, you must hear about the day *before* it was written.

CHAPTER 27

Paul said, "Tomorrow I write to Corinth. But I have asked all of you young men to sit with me today. We are going to take a look at the problems facing the church in Corinth. I want you all to know that the problems in Corinth will be similar to those you will find in churches you will work with the rest of your lives.

"Listen to this list of questions! How would *you* answer these questions?" Paul glanced around the room.

As I listened to Paul read the questions, I felt more and more hopeless for Corinth. Before he finished, we all despaired.

When he finished, Paul did something so typical of him: He seized the opportunity afforded by Corinth's problems to teach us. He always sought to show us the deeper issues, to find the underlying cause of a problem, *not* the surface issue.

Paul turned first to Secundus. "What is the greatest single problem you see in Corinth?" he asked.

Secundus did not hesitate. "The church in Corinth needs to know who Paul is. Do you have a *special* relationship with Corinth? Or are you simply what Peter and Apollos are to Corinth? Are you one of several workers who come to Corinth? To whom do they ultimately look? Is it you?"

(I look back on that moment and realize the question Secundus posed was probably the hardest question, the most frequently asked question, as well as the question that, when asked in the churches, caused more problems and damaged more churches than any other. I know this to be true because the men in that room traveled all across Syria, Cilicia, Asia Minor, Italy, and Crete. And wherever we carried on the Lord's work, this question came up: "Just who are *you*, anyway?")

"Gaius? What do you see as the major problem in Corinth?" asked Paul.

Gaius, always quick, answered, "The greatest single question causing the greatest amount of problems in Corinth is: Why does Paul not take money?"

I choked! Titus slapped his forehead. Paul murmured something. (I think he said: "Should I live so long to have such a question asked of me!") But Gaius was more right than we realized.

Paul considered Gaius's answer for a moment.

"Blastinius raised that same question in Galatia: 'Why is it Paul will not take money? *Why* is this?' "

"People begin to think you are rich, Paul," said Gaius. "First, they think you do not need money. Then they get jealous because you are so rich—they want *you* to give *them* money. All I can tell you is that not asking for money creates a stumbling block to a large number of people."

Paul shook his head in dismay. "Amazing. Amazing. But true. This has caused *great* trouble in all the Gentile churches."

Then Paul laughed! "Me, rich? Look at my clothes. Do they look like the clothes of a wealthy man?"

We all stared at Paul's clothes.

"They look more like the clothes of a runaway slave," teased Titus.

"I seem to be well known everywhere, and yet I am also

unknown. I made many rich, but in all this world I do not have five denarii. I have gained *nothing* from the gospel. What you see on my back is all the clothes I have in this world, except, of course, for my Pharisee garb, and I wear that only when I go to a synagogue. As for that five denarii—that is money I *earned* in the marketplace. Working hard, very hard."

Paul glared around the room again. Then, mischievously, he spoke in mock indignation: "And those five denarii will go to feed the young men I brought here to Ephesus."

Then, showing the seriousness that he held in his heart, he added, "Every day in the marketplace I am underbid by slaves whose masters send them into the market with orders to underbid *all free men*. This seems to be especially true of those in the business of tentmaking.

"Some days I sit in the marketplace and never earn so much as a mite. As you know, there are days when we gather here at Tyrannus's school and fast. We do so because we have little or no food. Yes, I am rich, but not in goods!"

"Then, Paul," insisted Aristarchus, "why, oh why, do you not take money?"

"For several reasons," answered Paul intensely. "First, so that no man can say that Paul of Tarsus makes money by the gospel. Or takes money from believers or from the assemblies. Second, that other workers in other places may never be able to criticize me in this area. Third, because every man who has ever served God has been open to criticism about money. Only the emperor in Rome gets criticized more."

Paul's brow furrowed, and his eyes blazed. "*Finally*," he exclaimed, "no man who gets paid for preaching the gospel can live without ending up with a shadow hanging over him. Many a man has wanted to say something to God's people but could not do so simply because he knew he might offend the Lord's people and, as a result, receive less money or no money at all. I have never had that chain on me, and I *never* will."

Paul breathed out ever so slowly and added, "Brothers, I say anything I want to, when I want to, where I want to, on any subject I desire—because I owe no man anything, and no man owns me. When there is fire in my belly, it is *never* quenched because of income. There is no income for me except what comes to me by my own two hands."

It was a ringing declaration that the men in that room never forgot.

Paul now turned to Sopater. "What do you consider the greatest problem or the greatest need in Corinth?"

"Paul," said Sopater, "it is true that the church is being ripped apart by the different camps . . . by favoritism that has grown up around Apollos, Peter, and you. *But* it is equally true that the church in Corinth is being ripped asunder by something else—by the *gifts.*"

I, Timothy, once more dropped my head in a feeling of utter hopelessness.

"Can any church have so many varied problems and still survive?" I said out loud.

"The gifts and tongues! The problems they are causing are as great as, or greater than, the schism between those camping around Apollos and Peter, and Paul."

There was a moment of silence. Tychicus and then Trophimus, wiser than the rest of us, had said nothing. Trophimus very hesitantly inquired, "Paul, what do you see as the most important problem facing Corinth?"

Paul, throwing his arms in the air, burst out, "Immorality! Of course, immorality!"

Then Paul looked at me. "Timothy, what do you consider to be the greatest problem in Corinth?"

"Under no circumstances am I going to place my head on

that chopping block. I confess ignorance. But be sure to ask my uncircumcised brother, Titus."

Titus took the challenge!

Trying his best to look Paul straight in the eye, Titus cleared his throat and said, "Ministry, brother Paul, ministry, ministry, and more ministry. Ministry that will bring these brothers and sisters *back to Christ* and get them off these ridiculous distractions! You have said the center is not 'what the ear hears nor the eye sees nor what the heart of man conceives.' Therefore, these *not* being the center, the center has to do with *things of the Spirit.* And the things of the Spirit are nothing less than *Christ!*"

The room fell silent.

"Hmmm" is all that Paul said in response to Titus, but he was thinking a great deal more.

"All of you have spoken well. One of you has spoken *very* well. Now! Tomorrow I write a letter to the Corinthians."

CHAPTER 28

This may take all day or perhaps even two days," said Paul.

"I have much to say to Corinth . . . and then . . . there are all those questions the Corinthians asked me to answer. Yes, perhaps *two* days."

It was a spring day in Ephesus and twenty-seven years since the Resurrection and Pentecost. Paul was about to write his fourth epistle to a church. (His other letters—so far—were to the four churches in Galatia and then two letters to the Christians in Thessalonica.)

There were four people in the room: Paul, Titus, Sosthenes of Corinth, and me. It fell to me, Timothy, to write down what Paul dictated. Sosthenes was invited to be present with the view that he would take the letter to Corinth, thereby vouching for its authenticity. Paul had planned to send me to Corinth shortly after Sosthenes delivered the letter.

Why did Paul not actually write with his own hand? He was well past forty years of age, and no man over forty could see well enough to write.

"I must be very careful," were Paul's first words. "There is a good possibility that some of the things I say may hurt many in Corinth. God's people are fragile . . . especially those causing the most problems! I must begin, therefore, by reminding them that they are holy ones even though very raw sin has been tolerated in the church . . . still, they *are* holy ones."

And so the letter began.

> This letter is from Paul, chosen by the will of God to be an apostle of Christ Jesus, and from our brother Sosthenes.
>
> We are writing to the church of God in Corinth, you who have been called by God to be his own holy people. He made you holy by means of Christ Jesus, just as he did all Christians everywhere—whoever calls upon the name of Jesus Christ, our Lord and theirs.
>
> May God our Father and the Lord Jesus Christ give you his grace and peace.

Paul paused, as he would many times during that day.

"Brothers, I love these dear Corinthians. I think of them every day and never stop thanking God for the ecclesia in Corinth—they are the joy, the consternation of my heart." Paul then mused, "So many gifts, so much knowledge. The results? They are fighting with one another like children!"

Paul shook his head slowly. We waited. Then he continued.

> I can never stop thanking God for all the generous gifts he has given you, now that you belong to Christ Jesus. He has enriched your church with the gifts of eloquence and every kind of knowledge. This shows that what I told you about Christ is true. Now you have every spiritual gift you need as you eagerly wait for the return of our Lord Jesus Christ. He will keep you strong right up to the end, and he will keep you free from all blame on the great day when our Lord Jesus Christ returns. God will surely do this for you, for he always does just what he says, and he is the one who invited you into this wonderful friendship with his Son, Jesus Christ our Lord.
>
> Now, dear brothers and sisters, I appeal to you by the

> authority of the Lord Jesus Christ to stop arguing among yourselves. Let there be real harmony so there won't be divisions in the church. I plead with you to be of one mind, united in thought and purpose.

Paul looked up. "I am so glad that Sebastian, of the house of Chloe, has given me permission to refer to the words that he and others from Corinth have shared with me. You three are all familiar with Chloe's household?"

"Yes," we replied, but Titus was a little hesitant.

"It is a large organization, founded perhaps two generations ago, by a family named Chloe. This company now does business all over the empire, especially the port cities of the Mediterranean. Sebastian, along with two or three other brothers in the ecclesia in Corinth, comes here to Ephesus frequently to buy and sell for that company. Sebastian has told me much about the mess in Corinth. I believe half of it!"

> For some members of Chloe's household have told me about your arguments, dear brothers and sisters.

Paul's eyes filled with tears. "Oh my, this is more difficult than I anticipated."

> Some of you are saying, "I am a follower of Paul." Others are saying, "I follow Apollos," or "I follow Peter," or "I follow only Christ." Can Christ be divided into pieces?
>
> Was I, Paul, crucified for you? Were any of you baptized in the name of Paul? I thank God that I did not baptize any of you except Crispus and Gaius, for now no one can say they were baptized in my name. (Oh yes, I also baptized the household of Stephanas. I don't remember baptizing anyone else.) For Christ didn't send me to baptize, but to preach the Good News—and not with clever speeches and high-sounding ideas, for fear that the cross of Christ would lose its power.

"Titus," sighed Paul. "You are not quite as familiar with the Greek mind as is Timothy. The power of the Greek is as strong in Corinth as it is anywhere in the world, *except* Athens. These Corinthian Greeks are born philosophers—they love to hear great orators. Greek orators leave the impression that they are very wise. They also leave the impression that they have made the people who hear them very wise.

"Both are given to the ear. As I said . . . and as you said . . . the ear is not the location of man's spirit. The Jews? Well, I will get into that matter a little later. Right now, I am far more concerned about the Greeks. The Greeks in the assembly in Corinth far outnumber both the Italians and the Jews. They love to hear their Greek ancestors quoted, to hear theories, and while they are speaking, they think they are proving just how wise they are. Faith means little to a Greek. The Cross makes no sense at all."

> I know very well how foolish the message of the cross sounds to those who are on the road to destruction. But we who are being saved recognize this message as the very power of God. As the Scriptures say, "I will destroy human wisdom and discard their most brilliant ideas."
>
> So where does this leave the philosophers, the scholars, and the world's brilliant debaters? God has made them all look foolish and has shown their wisdom to be useless nonsense. Since God in his wisdom saw to it that the world would never find him through human wisdom, he has used our foolish preaching to save all who believe. God's way seems foolish to the Jews because they want a sign from heaven to prove it is true. And it is foolish to the Greeks because they believe only what agrees with their own wisdom. So when we preach that Christ was crucified, the Jews are offended, and the Gentiles say it's all nonsense. But to those called by God to salvation, both Jews and Gentiles, Christ is the mighty power of God and the wonderful wis-

> dom of God. This "foolish" plan of God is far wiser than the wisest of human plans, and God's weakness is far stronger than the greatest of human strength.

Paul leaned back and looked over at Titus again.

"It is quite amazing. Most of the Greek believers in Corinth cannot read or write. The majority are slaves, and the majority of the non-Greek believers are also freed slaves. Yet those illiterate Greeks are very prideful. It seems almost all Greeks see themselves as wise, and yet it is only because of the speeches they hear.

"Apollos, with his great oratorical skills, has not helped this situation at all."

> Remember, dear brothers and sisters, that few of you were wise in the world's eyes, or powerful, or wealthy when God called you. Instead, God deliberately chose things the world considers foolish in order to shame those who think they are wise. And he chose those who are powerless to shame those who are powerful. God chose things despised by the world, things counted as nothing at all, and used them to bring to nothing what the world considers important, so that no one can ever boast in the presence of God.
>
> God alone made it possible for you to be in Christ Jesus. For our benefit God made Christ to be wisdom itself. He is the one who made us acceptable to God. He made us pure and holy, and he gave himself to purchase our freedom.

"The prophet Jeremiah said something that addressed this very issue." Paul then quoted Jeremiah:

> As the Scriptures say, "The person who wishes to boast should boast only of what the Lord has done."

"Dare I say anything about Apollos directly? If I do, I will hurt many. He came to Corinth with such brilliance. I came with nothing but Christ, and *him* dying on the cross. The Corinthians took my lack of oratorical skills as a sign of weakness." Paul smiled. "It did not help that my Greek is very rough. . . . I did not have the skills to speak in Greek as I should. I certainly do not have Apollos's skills. To the Greeks, it is an insult to speak publicly in Greek unless it is spoken perfectly. Nonetheless, with only the poorest of Greek, the power of God did come through. The Corinthians seem to have forgotten that! Forgotten the power of God to salvation . . . the greatest of all demonstrations of power.

"Brothers, I tell you the truth, in those days if there had been some believers in Corinth who were mature in Christ, perhaps I could even have spoken with *wisdom;* but even then it would have been the wisdom of God . . . even the secrets of the very heart and mind of the Lord himself. But the Greeks want their ears filled! The Jews . . . ah . . . they want proof God exists! Miracles! Did not Isaiah also have something to say about this? 'Neither the eye, nor ear, nor imagination can grasp what God has prepared for his children.' Only the spirit can."

Paul ended this subject with these words from Isaiah:

> No eye has seen, nor ear has heard, and no mind has imagined,
> what God has prepared for those who love him.

Paul turned again to Titus. "Titus, if it is not what the ear hears, nor eye sees, nor the imagination conceives, then how do we know the things that are prepared for those of us who love God?"

"Why do you keep asking me questions? Timothy is in this room too!"

"Answer, Titus."

Titus's words came back like an arrow. "Because we have a spirit. The Lord's Spirit has entered into our spirit and become one with us. Things of the spirit have nothing to do with the flesh. The flesh does not know, and certainly the ear of the soul and the eye of the soul do not know. It is only what is buried deep within us—the Spirit—who can know the mind of God."

(Titus was shaking all over by the time he finished.)

"Thank you, Titus." Paul was obviously pleased. "May I quote your words to the Corinthians?"

Titus frowned. "*My* words! You know I learned everything I know from *you!*"

"Not so," replied Paul. "Most of what you know of Christ you learned from him . . . him who indwells you."

Having said that, Paul motioned for me to write again. And Titus listened intently.

> But we know these things because God has revealed them to us by his Spirit, and his Spirit searches out everything and shows us even God's deep secrets.

Titus glowed.

Paul continued dictating, speaking further about God's Spirit and contrasting the ways of the Spirit with the ways of man.

> But people who aren't Christians can't understand these truths from God's Spirit. It all sounds foolish to them because only those who have the Spirit can understand what the Spirit means.

After Paul had dictated a bit more, he paused. "I believe Isaiah had something more to say to us about these matters." Once more Paul quoted the ancient prophet.

> Who can know what the Lord is thinking? Who can give him counsel?

Paul added one more sentence. As I was writing it down I glanced up to see what seemed to be a shadow falling across Paul's face. There was a tear in Paul's eye.

"Now I must say some things I do not wish to say. I must address this problem that Apollos has nurtured into a crisis."

> Dear brothers and sisters, when I was with you I couldn't talk to you as I would to mature Christians. I had to talk as though you belonged to this world or as though you were infants in the Christian life. I had to feed you with milk and not with solid food, because you couldn't handle anything stronger. And you still aren't ready, for you are still controlled by your own sinful desires. You are jealous of one another and quarrel with each other. Doesn't that prove you are controlled by your own desires? You are acting like people who don't belong to the Lord. When one of you says, "I am a follower of Paul," and another says, "I prefer Apollos," aren't you acting like those who are not Christians?
>
> Who is Apollos, and who is Paul, that we should be the cause of such quarrels? Why, we're only servants. Through us God caused you to believe. Each of us did the work the Lord gave us.

"Listen to me, Titus, Timothy. You also, Sosthenes. The Corinthians do not realize that when I came into Corinth, I raised up the church. Apollos watered that church. But neither one of us really did anything. *God* is the one who brought forth the growth. God is the important one. *This*, the Corinthians do *not* understand. I would the Corinthians could see the partnership that has gone on between Apollos and me: One of us laid the foundation, and the other built upon it. Either way, the Corinthians are the building that is growing."

Paul stared into my eyes. "The Corinthians, and Apollos also, do not understand that wherever a man raises up a church, when another man comes, he must honor the work of the one who laid the foundation. He should be careful how he builds on someone else's foundation."

There was an edge in Paul's voice. "This is why I do *not* build on other men's foundations. . . . I go where the word of God has never been preached. Others build on the foundation I lay, yes—and often they are not careful. But, ah, even if he builds carelessly, that is acceptable. For any man who goes forth and raises up a church, a day will come when there will be a crisis in that church. A crisis has now come to Corinth. Peter came and built upon the foundation I laid. Apollos, perhaps not as careful as Peter, has also built upon the foundation I laid. There is one thing certain: There will never be a church raised up but that one day fire must fall upon that church *and* on the work of the man who laid the foundation. That day has come in Corinth, just as it did with four churches in Galatia *and* the churches in Philippi."

Paul signaled to me to write.

> Because of God's special favor to me, I have laid the foundation like an expert builder. Now others are building on it. But whoever is building on this foundation must be very careful.

Titus and I were surprised at the intensity with which Paul spoke. Oblivious to us, he continued.

> For no one can lay any other foundation than the one we already have—Jesus Christ. Now anyone who builds on that foundation may use gold, silver, jewels, wood, hay, or straw. But there is going to come a time of testing at the judgment day to see what kind of work each builder has done. Everyone's work will be put through the fire to see whether or not it keeps its value. If the work survives the fire, that builder will receive a reward. But if the work is burned up, the builder will suffer great loss. The builders themselves will be saved, but like someone escaping through a wall of flames.

Paul then spoke to the Corinthians about their being the temple of God. And that the holy of holies was within *them.*

"Corinthians seem not to understand even the most simple things."

Paul was speaking very fast now.

> Stop fooling yourselves. If you think you are wise by this world's standards, you will have to become a fool so you can become wise by God's standards.

Paul then quoted Job.

> For the wisdom of this world is foolishness to God. As the Scriptures say, "God catches those who think they are wise in their own cleverness."

He followed by a quotation out of Psalm 94.

> And again, 'The Lord knows the thoughts of the wise, that they are worthless.'

I was about to lay down my pen, awaiting Paul to choose his next subject. But Paul had much more to say on *this* subject.

> So don't take pride in following a particular leader. Everything belongs to you: Paul and Apollos and Peter; the whole world and life and death; the present and the future. Everything belongs to you, and you belong to Christ, and Christ belongs to God.

I was quite taken aback by how much Paul was saying about those who are involved in the Lord's work—specifically, planting churches.

> Our dedication to Christ makes us look like fools, but you are so wise! We are weak, but you are so powerful! You are well thought of, but we are laughed at. To this very hour we go hungry and thirsty, without enough clothes to keep us warm.

> We have endured many beatings, and we have no homes of our own. We have worked wearily with our own hands to earn our living. We bless those who curse us. We are patient with those who abuse us. We respond gently when evil things are said about us. Yet we are treated like the world's garbage, like everybody's trash—right up to the present moment.
>
> I am not writing these things to shame you, but to warn you as my beloved children. For even if you had ten thousand others to teach you about Christ, you have only one spiritual father. For I became your father in Christ Jesus when I preached the Good News to you. So I ask you to follow my example and do as I do.

"Sosthenes, you will be going to Corinth. Take this letter. Shortly, I will send Timothy to report back to me concerning the condition of the gathering in Corinth.

"Timothy, when you go to Corinth, I want you to make it very clear to those who say that I am weak and those who say that I have promised on several occasions to come to Corinth—but never get there . . . " Paul motioned for me to continue writing.

> I know that some of you have become arrogant, thinking I will never visit you again. But I will come—and soon—if the Lord will let me, and then I'll find out whether these arrogant people are just big talkers or whether they really have God's power. For the Kingdom of God is not just fancy talk; it is living by God's power. Which do you choose? Should I come with punishment and scolding, or should I come with quiet love and gentleness?

It was at *this* point that Paul decided to broach another subject: "Now let us deal with the problem of immorality," he announced. But what followed was the longest pause of silence in the entire day.

When Paul finally spoke, his voice was shaking.

"This matter of sexual immorality. This matter of a man living with his father's wife—and *no one* saying anything about it or *doing* anything about it." Paul spoke out as strongly as perhaps he ever spoke in addressing this matter. (I found it difficult to keep up.) This time Paul gave the church *orders*, a thing he rarely did. "Call a meeting, and cast the man out of the assembly and into the hands of Satan."

Again, I thought Paul had come to the end of the subject:

> It isn't my responsibility to judge outsiders, but it certainly is your job to judge those inside the church who are sinning in these ways. God will judge those on the outside; but as the Scriptures say, "You must remove the evil person from among you."

Another long pause ensued. Then, almost as if another person were speaking, Paul turned to the matter of lawsuits. (A few minutes later he returned to the subject of morals.)

"Titus, you need to know that it *seems* that everyone in Corinth had at one time or another sued at least one other person. This is because of the nature of the city. It is a place of much trade—too many languages, too many cultures, and therefore too many misunderstandings. As a consequence, the courts in Corinth are constantly flooded with lawsuits. But for a Christian to sue another believer?!"

Paul launched into this subject with a fury.

A few minutes later Priscilla came to the door. Paul invited her in. She served us pomegranate juice and honey-sweetened bread. Soon Paul was completely refreshed.

"Look at this question," he exclaimed. "It is not *one* question. It is a dozen. Marriage. Singles. Single men. Single women. Betrothed. Husbands. Wives. Widows. Everything imaginable about marital situations plus relations between husband and wives . . . and more."

His words resounded with frustration, but there was a twinkle in his eye.

> Now about the questions you asked in your letter. Yes, it is good to live a celibate life.

Paul set about answering all these questions, spending more time on these subjects than any others they asked. He ended abruptly and, without pausing, went right into the issue that had divided two brothers in the assembly, one a vegetarian and the other a meat eater.

The problem began at a butcher's shop in a Corinthian market. (The butcher's name is Lucius. He owns the largest meat market in Corinth.) I am still amazed at how many truths Paul was able to draw from this incident. As he came toward the end of the subject, he summoned up his thoughts in these words:

> But you must be careful with this freedom of yours. Do not cause a brother or sister with a weaker conscience to stumble.
>
> You see, this is what can happen: Weak Christians who think it is wrong to eat this food will see you eating in the temple of an idol. You know there's nothing wrong with it, but they will be encouraged to violate their conscience by eating food that has been dedicated to the idol. So because of your superior knowledge, a weak Christian, for whom Christ died, will be destroyed. And you are sinning against Christ when you sin against other Christians by encouraging them to do something they believe is wrong. If what I eat is going to make another Christian sin, I will never eat meat again as long as I live—for I don't want to make another Christian stumble.

Priscilla returned, this time with the noon meal. While the rest of us ate, Paul became lost in thought. When he began again, the list of questions was completely laid aside. Paul had been reflecting on some of the criticisms that brothers in the Corinthian assembly had laid against him. Resuming his dictation, he spoke of himself and Barnabas—that they had given their whole lives only to Jesus Christ. He spoke very bluntly about the fact that he would not accept money and that some in Corinth had criticized him for that fact.

> Do I not have as much freedom as anyone else? Am I not an apostle? Haven't I seen Jesus our Lord with my own eyes? Isn't it because of my hard work that you are in the Lord? Even if others think I am not an apostle, I certainly am to you, for you are living proof that I am the Lord's apostle.
>
> This is my answer to those who question my authority as an apostle. Don't we have the right to live in your homes and share your meals? Don't we have the right to bring a Christian wife along with us as the other disciples and the Lord's brothers and Peter do? Or is it only Barnabas and I who have to work to support ourselves?

Once his words seemed to be directed to someone who was Jewish:

> For the law of Moses says, "Do not keep an ox from eating as it treads out the grain." Do you suppose God was thinking only about oxen when he said this? Wasn't he also speaking to us? Of course he was. Just as farm workers who plow fields and thresh the grain expect a share of the harvest, Christian workers should be paid by those they serve.
>
> We have planted good spiritual seed among you. Is it too much to ask, in return, for mere food and clothing? If you support others who preach to you, shouldn't we have an even greater right to be supported?

The direction of Paul's words abruptly changed.

> Yet we have never used this right. We would rather put up with anything than put an obstacle in the way of the Good News about Christ.

Paul used another illustration, this time about the priests in the Temple—that *they* ate the food offered on the altar in Jerusalem. He made it clear that these priests received a share of the sacrificial offering. He also quoted the Lord as saying that those who preached the gospel should benefit from the fact that they preached the gospel. There was a moment when I thought Paul might be changing his own personal convictions about money and would begin accepting pay! Was I wrong!

> Yet I have never used any of these rights[!] And I am not writing this to suggest that I would like to start now[!] In fact, I would rather die than lose my distinction of preaching without charge.

I tried very hard to keep from laughing, but Paul was speaking fast, and they were words charged with conviction. (I did not stop, but I was amused.)

> For preaching the Good News is not something I can boast about. I am compelled by God to do it. How terrible for me if I didn't do it!
>
> If I were doing this of my own free will, then I would deserve payment. But God has chosen me and given me this sacred trust, and I have no choice. What then is my pay? It is the satisfaction I get from preaching the Good News without expense to anyone, never demanding my rights as a preacher.

Paul then stated in one sentence the main reason he did not take money:

> This means I am not bound to obey people just because they pay me[!], yet I have become a servant of everyone so that I can bring them to Christ.

Here was a man who was raising the standard of the worker far higher than other men who had come before him.

He ended his reflections by saying,

> I discipline my body like an athlete, training it to do what it should. Otherwise, I fear that after preaching to others I myself might be disqualified.

By now Paul had completely forgotten about the list of questions. He had moved totally off those inquiries and had poured out his heart. Instead, he had released some of the pain buried deep within him . . . but always with a view to helping the Corinthians understand spiritual things in a higher way.

Paul then turned to a more general subject—the walk of the church itself. He spoke not so much to the individual as he did to the *corporate body*. He spoke to the assembly as if the assembly were a person.

He graphically reminded the Corinthians of what had happened in the wilderness long ago when there was rebellion against Moses.

> These events happened as a warning to us, so that we would not crave evil things as they did or worship idols as some of them did.

Titus and I both wanted very much to interrupt Paul and discuss this incident with him. He could tell we did, but he did not stop. Yet I sensed a certain satisfaction on his part, knowing that if he was getting through to us, he would surely get through to the Corinthians.

We were arrested as we realized that events that happened hundreds of years ago happened to warn *us!*

Paul reiterated his point emphatically:

> All these events happened to them as examples for us. They were written down to warn us, who live at the time when this age is drawing to a close[!]

Paul followed this passage with a plea to the Corinthians, imploring them to flee from idol worship.

> What am I trying to say? Am I saying that the idols to whom the pagans bring sacrifices are real gods and that these sacrifices are of some value? No, not at all. What I am saying is that these sacrifices are offered to demons, not to God.

When I heard Paul say these words, I dropped my pen. "Demons!"

A discussion followed. Again, I could see the light in Paul's eyes as he watched the young men he was training begin to learn new things of which they knew nothing.

I expected Paul to continue his present line of thought. Instead he returned to the earlier issue of vegetarians and meat eaters.

> Here's what you should do. You may eat any meat that is sold in the marketplace. Don't ask whether or not it was offered to idols, and then your conscience won't be bothered.

Here Paul quoted Psalm 24.

> For "the earth is the Lord's, and everything in it."

He continued on with the subject a little longer, speaking about what to do if an unbeliever invites you to a meal. I felt Paul had reached some very high, lofty ideals, but not one of us in the room would forget what Paul had to say as he completed his thought.

> Now, why should my freedom be limited by what someone else thinks? If I can thank God for the food and enjoy it, why

> should I be condemned for eating it? Whatever you eat or drink or whatever you do, you must do all for the glory of God. Don't give offense to Jews or Gentiles or the church of God. That is the plan I follow, too. I try to please everyone in everything I do. I don't just do what I like or what is best for me, but what is best for them so they may be saved.

The next question Paul answered was one we all dreaded. It had to do with hair. Someone was certain to be offended.

"This issue does not surprise me—but there is no solution! Cultures are clashing in Corinth. When it comes to culture, no one understands the other person's cultural view."

Paul continued, "Let me explain the problem. The Orientals in Corinth want *all* women in the assembly to cover their heads. That is because *all* Oriental women do! The Greeks, on the other hand, want all the unmarried women *not* to cover their heads . . . but the married women to cover theirs. This is a Greek custom. The Roman women who are in the church in Corinth will have none of this. They insist that *none* of the women ever cover their heads because *Italian* women *never* cover their heads.

"The Jews have been pulled into the argument, but only as to what is a woman's place in the church. They insist she is subservient to man because man came before woman, and woman came out of man. And *that* is a Jewish teaching. Scripture? I will let you three brothers better decide that for yourselves. I remember when Gamaliel taught this idea to me. But it was all based on logic decided from one man's interpretation of Scripture.

"There is another view, of course—a higher one."

Paul smiled.

"The Jews say woman came from man. They fail to mention that—ever since then—every man has come out of woman.

"As you can see, I am actually being asked two questions: First, the Corinthians want to know what the custom is in the other Gentile churches! Well, the other churches never even had a thought about this subject! Second, the Corinthians want *my* opinion. *Should a woman cover her head?* I have no opinion. But I suppose I should have one."

Paul dove into the subject, quoting some of the teachings about what the Jews thought and what the Greeks thought.

There is an old saying that man was not made for woman's benefit, but woman was made for man's benefit. Paul quoted that and then turned it, giving a view from the standpoint of the new creation. Not the view of the old creation, nor the view of the Jews, nor the view of the Greeks.

> But in relationships among the Lord's people, women are not independent of men, and men are not independent of women.

Paul then added emphatically,

> . . . and everything comes from God.

"What do the other Gentile churches teach about women covering or *not* covering their heads? Can the Greeks not understand that the other churches do not think about such issues?"

After a pause that seemed to contain a mingling of sadness and humor, Paul looked at the next question. I could tell the question irritated Paul.

Paul laid aside the list.

"Remember what the brothers from Corinth told us? I speak of the Lord's meal."

Hearing this, all three of us dropped our heads.

"That meal," groaned Sosthenes.

In our hearts we had hoped Paul would not even address that incident . . . a shameful incident that had to do with an evening meal the assembly took together.

We have no idea what kind of meeting it had been, but this we knew: Some got drunk! Some overate. Some had no food at all.

The tragedy is that the Lord's Supper was taken right in the middle of all this shameful conduct. Paul was both saddened and furious. And embarrassed. We were not at all surprised that his words were terse and plain:

> So, dear brothers and sisters, when you gather for the Lord's Supper, wait for each other. If you are really hungry, eat at home so you won't bring judgment upon yourselves when you meet together.

When Paul finished, he was spent. He glanced at the list once more, then stood.

"This is enough. I am not going to answer any more questions. . . . I will wait until I get to Corinth and answer this question in their presence." With that, Paul began to move toward the door.

"Paul, if you are not going to answer the rest of the questions, should you not tell them so?" Sosthenes asked.

"Oh yes, of course!" Paul looked at me and said the following,

> I'll give you instructions about the other matters after I arrive.

Once more Paul turned toward the door. "It is a beautiful day. Let us step out of the city for a while and walk in the fields."

It was afternoon.

I, Timothy, had no idea that when we returned Paul would unfold the most beautiful poem—in Greek!—anyone had ever heard. (Who said Apollos was more articulate than Paul?)

You will find it interesting to discover the source of this incredibly beautiful poem.

CHAPTER 29

Sit down, please," invited Paul. "I believe we can now finish this letter before night.

"It is now time that I address some of the Corinthians' misunderstandings about the gifts. I am not so sure all those gifts of theirs are operating as beautifully as they think." (Paul was referring to the rowdy Corinthian meetings, which, like that dinner, sometimes got out of control!)

Paul explained that several times chaos had broken out in the meetings, with two or three people talking all at one time, while others were speaking in tongues. Beyond that, unfortunately there was hardly anyone in the ecclesia in Corinth who could actually minister Christ to others. Certainly not the way that Paul or Peter (or even Apollos) had done.

To add to the chaos, translators were often present in the meetings because so many languages were represented in the gatherings. Add to that, glossolalia. Several people would talk at the same time, others in tongues, and added to that were the low voices of translators . . . the result was chaos. Yes, often joyful chaos, but chaos nonetheless. As to glossolalia, it could be beautiful, but at other times it was completely out of control.

"Now add to this one, *pride.* Some feel they have a *special* gift—a gift better than others have. It is a short leap from believing you have a special gift to also believing—therefore—that you *are* special."

Even as I wrote down what Paul was saying, I was surprised—as often I have been—at the way he handled problems within an assembly. Paul's use of the illustration of the human body in comparison to the body of Christ—the church—was one of the most helpful things Paul ever wrote to a church experiencing internal problems. Coming to a close, he presented a stirring exhortation. His words were eloquent.

> Now all of you together are Christ's body, and each one of you is a separate and necessary part of it. Here is a list of some of the members that God has placed in the body of Christ:
>
> first are apostles,
> second are prophets,
> third are teachers,
> then those who do miracles,
> those who have the gift of healing,
> those who can help others,
> those who can get others to work together,
> those who speak in unknown languages.
>
> Is everyone an apostle? Of course not. Is everyone a prophet? No. Are all teachers? Does everyone have the power to do miracles? Does everyone have the gift of healing? Of course not. Does God give all of us the ability to speak in unknown languages? Can everyone interpret unknown languages? No!

Having said the words, Paul leaned back against the wall, closed his eyes, and then added,

> In any event, you should desire the most helpful gifts. First, however, let me tell you about something else that is better than any of them!

What followed *was* poetry, perhaps the most beautiful poetry ever written in the Greek language. All three of us knew something special was going to happen, but we had no idea what!

Something better than any of the gifts. What will Paul say? I thought.

Suddenly Paul began to sing! In Greek. It was a poem. A majestic poem. Only Titus recognized it, yet even he had heard Paul sing it only once.

"Paul wrote this poem just a few days after his salvation. It was written at a time when Paul laid aside—forever—his legalism," whispered Titus.

When Paul finished, we were all weeping.

"I will repeat these lines, Timothy. As I do, write them down."

> If I could speak in any language in heaven or on earth but didn't love others, I would only be making meaningless noise like a loud gong or a clanging cymbal. If I had the gift of prophecy, and if I knew all the mysteries of the future and knew everything about everything, but didn't love others, what good would I be? And if I had the gift of faith so that I could speak to a mountain and make it move, without love I would be no good to anybody.

At that moment I realized Paul was addressing the central issue existing in the Corinthian assembly.

> And if I had the gift of faith so that I could speak to a mountain and make it move, without love I would be no good to anybody. If I gave everything I have to the poor and even sacrificed my body, I could boast about it; but if I didn't love others, I would be of no value whatsoever.
>
> Love is patient and kind. Love is not jealous or boastful or proud or rude. Love does not demand its own way. Love is not irritable, and it keeps no record of when it has been wronged. It is never glad about injustice but rejoices

> whenever the truth wins out. Love never gives up, never loses faith, is always hopeful, and endures through every circumstance.
>
> Love will last forever, but prophecy and speaking in unknown languages and special knowledge will all disappear. Now we know only a little, and even the gift of prophecy reveals little! But when the end comes, these special gifts will all disappear.
>
> It's like this: When I was a child, I spoke and thought and reasoned as a child does. But when I grew up, I put away childish things. Now we see things imperfectly as in a poor mirror, but then we will see everything with perfect clarity. All that I know now is partial and incomplete, but then I will know everything completely, just as God knows me now. There are three things that will endure—faith, hope, and love—and the greatest of these is love.

I looked up and noticed Titus's eyes were red from crying.

"So much for Apollos's eloquence!" choked Sosthenes. "Titus, will you sing it with Paul?" he asked.

"Absolutely not," rejoined Titus, "but I will join *you* in singing it." And so the four of us sang the song together. When we were finished, we fell on our faces and poured our hearts out to the Lord. None more than Paul.

It was an hour before Paul said anything else. I would have thought that our brother could reach no higher. This time Paul addressed the fact that there were not enough people in the Corinthian gathering who could stand up on their feet and proclaim Jesus Christ. Paul pointed out that to have *that* ministry in the gatherings would strengthen the entire church.

Once more Paul chose perfect words.

> Dear brothers and sisters, if I should come to you talking in an unknown language, how would that help you? But if I bring you some revelation or some special knowledge or some prophecy or some teaching—that is what will help you. Even

> musical instruments like the flute or the harp, though they are lifeless, are examples of the need for speaking in plain language. For no one will recognize the melody unless the notes are played clearly. And if the bugler doesn't sound a clear call, how will the soldiers know they are being called to battle? And it's the same for you. If you talk to people in a language they don't understand, how will they know what you mean? You might as well be talking to an empty room.

The assembly in Corinth was a collision of many cultures and languages. Further, there were many visitors—as one might expect in a city receiving dozens of ships at its docks every day, not to mention local people who came to the gatherings out of curiosity. Paul implored the assembly not to let a meeting get out of order because if some local person walked into the assembly, he would think he had stepped into some foreign country.

This reflected a conviction strongly held by Paul. He recalled vividly how when a Gentile walked into a gathering of Jewish believers in Cyprus, he felt as if he had walked into a foreign country—*Israel!* Over and over again Paul had said to the assemblies, "Every church ought to be unique, springing up out of the local soil. The church should reflect the local culture. When those who are born and raised in the city come to your meetings, they should not feel they have suddenly entered a foreign culture."

In the midst of this exhortation, Paul again quoted Isaiah.

> "I will speak to my own people through unknown languages and through the lips of foreigners. But even then, they will not listen to me," says the Lord.

He then continued on with the most practical of advice. How that man could be so practical and so spiritual at the same time is beyond me! In my judgment, Paul of Tarsus was the perfect Christian worker, capable of addressing all issues on all fronts . . . giving practical and spiritual solutions as though they were one.

Paul smiled. "If Priscilla lived in Corinth, I would say that *she* asked this next question."

"Does it have to do with synagogues?" asked a laughing Titus.

"No," replied Paul, "but something similar. Tell me, Titus, have you ever heard of a law in Syria that says a woman cannot speak in a public square—at a gathering of the townspeople?"

"Of course not," replied Titus, a little cautious at such an odd question. "We Jews love laws. We have hundreds upon hundreds of them, but we do not prohibit a woman from speaking in a gathering at the city gate. After all, we Jews had a judge named Deborah. She not only spoke at the gatherings at the city gate but also ruled over those gatherings!"

"Ah, but the Greeks, they have a law!" said Paul. "Women do not speak in such gatherings. It goes like this: The city council comes out to the city square and calls out: 'Ecclesia! Ecclesia! Assembly! Assembly!' All the men who care to, walk to the marketplace and gather around the bema. Then begins a talkfest. The ecclesia goes on for hours . . . sometimes all day . . . with man after man asking questions and making speeches."

"And the women can't say anything?" asked Titus.

"Not a word! Not even a *whisper* to their husbands! In the secular and governmental ecclesia a woman must not speak. For her to speak in such an assembly is to disgrace her husband.

"But there are many Roman women in Corinth, Greece! They are angry at the Greeks for not letting women speak. Now here is the question—I shall read it to you: 'We believers are free from all law. Therefore, are we women free to break Greek law and speak out in the secular ecclesia? Can't we at least ask questions in the ecclesia the government calls? After all, women can speak in the *Lord's* ecclesia—why not *man's* ecclesia?' "

"It sounds like a reasonable question to me," replied Titus, who then added lightly, "If a woman *does* speak out in the forum, will they send her to jail? It seems to me that if a believing woman is willing to go to jail for talking in the assembly, she should do so."

"No such punishment," replied Paul. "It is just that she has disgraced her husband. You can imagine how a Roman husband takes to being disgraced in a Greek ecclesia!"

Very patiently Paul dictated his answer, explaining why a woman—who *can* speak in the Lord's assembly—should obey Greek law and not speak out in man's assembly.

Having finished, Paul once more changed the subject abruptly and pointedly. His next words were blunt. He addressed those people who felt they had a special gift from God. These particular people were puffed up about their spiritual abilities and were causing much trouble as a result. (One brother saw himself as a speaker—a *better one* than Paul. He had become very conceited about his speaking ability and was trying to get the church to follow Apollos and not Paul.)

Paul closed with these words:

> If you claim to be a prophet or think you are very spiritual, you should recognize that what I am saying is a command from the Lord himself. But if you do not recognize this, you will not be recognized.
>
> So, dear brothers and sisters, be eager to prophesy, and don't forbid speaking in tongues. But be sure that everything is done properly and in order.

"One last matter to cover," said Paul. "It seems I have made the same mistake in Corinth as I did in Thessalonica. I have failed to say anything about the resurrection. One of the things that brought confusion to the assembly in Thessalonica came about because I neglected this subject. I must now speak of the resurrection of Christ lest the same thing happen again. What kind of bodies shall we expect our resurrected ones to be?"

I, Timothy, say to you, if you should ever read a copy of the letter of Paul to the Corinthians, by all means pay close attention to this passage. Here Paul speaks of the day when God shall be all . . . and in all.

Paul spoke so splendidly about the Lord Jesus, about *his* resurrected body *and* ours! He then informed the Corinthians as to what it would be like at the time of the resurrection of the redeemed.

I must share my own prejudice. Of everything Paul wrote that day, the most profound and mysterious were these words from Psalm 8:

> And the last enemy to be destroyed is death. For the Scriptures say, "God has given him authority over all things." (Of course, when it says "authority over all things," it does not include God himself, who gave Christ his authority.) Then, when he has conquered all things, the Son will present himself to God, so that God, who gave his Son authority over all things, will be utterly supreme over everything everywhere.

This passage has been the guiding light of all that I, Timothy, have proclaimed to God's people.

Paul moved on to speak of the glorified bodies that we will receive when we rise from the dead. In the midst of this declaration, Paul quoted from Genesis 2:

> The first man, Adam, became a living person. But the last Adam—that is, Christ—is a life-giving Spirit.

Paul ended this part of his letter with these resounding words:

> When this happens—when our perishable earthly bodies have been transformed into heavenly bodies that will never die—then at last the Scriptures will come true:

"Death is swallowed up in victory.
O death, where is your victory?
O death, where is your sting?"

For sin is the sting that results in death, and the law gives sin its power. How we thank God, who gives us victory over sin and death through Jesus Christ our Lord!

So, my dear brothers and sisters, be strong and steady, always enthusiastic about the Lord's work, for you know that nothing you do for the Lord is ever useless.

If you look at the very end of Paul's letters, you will notice that he always closes with very practical words. On this occasion he gave instructions concerning the famine in Israel and the suffering of the poor believers in Jerusalem.

At the time Peter was in Corinth, he had told the believers there about the plight of the older people in Jerusalem. The church in Corinth immediately responded. After that, the drought in Israel became even more acute—so much so that Paul asked all the Gentile churches to send help to Jerusalem. He had gone so far as to write a letter to all the Gentile churches asking them to put aside an amount of money to take to Jerusalem. Because Corinth was the very first assembly to make a promise to help, Paul looked to them to set an example to the other Gentile churches in their raising of money.

Now about the money being collected for the Christians in Jerusalem: You should follow the same procedures I gave to the churches in Galatia. On every Lord's Day, each of you should put aside some amount of money in relation to what you have earned and save it for this offering. Don't wait until I get there and then try to collect it all at once. When I come I will write letters of recommendation for the messengers you choose to deliver your gift to Jerusalem. And if it seems appropriate for me also to go along, then we can travel together.

Unwittingly, Paul's next statement did not sit well with many in Corinth. He explained that he had planned to leave Ephesus and go into northern Greece and that he would remain there for a while—perhaps the entire winter. Then he would come south to Corinth. (The Jewish festival of Pentecost was approaching, and Paul wanted to stay in Ephesus until this festival because of the wide open door to the gospel. Then he would go to Philippi. He was later criticized by a few for saying he would soon be in Corinth and for not keeping his word.)

With that, Paul touched on the subject of Apollos—and in a very positive way. (I suspect that this was difficult for Paul to do, but he was ever the gracious man.) Then Paul added:

> You know that Stephanas and his household were the first to become Christians in Greece, and they are spending their lives in service to other Christians. I urge you, dear brothers and sisters, to respect them fully and others like them who serve with such real devotion. I am so glad that Stephanas, Fortunatus, and Achaicus have come here. They have been making up for the help you weren't here to give me.

Was Paul saying that it would have been good, when he first arrived in Ephesus, to have brothers and sisters from the other churches come and help with the beginning? Or was he speaking of the fact that Corinth never sent any money to help in the work in Ephesus? I do not know.

> They have been a wonderful encouragement to me, as they have been to you, too. You must give proper honor to all who serve so well.

The ending of a letter was always difficult for Paul. It was as though, in closing a letter, he had to end his fellowship with that church.

Paul's final greetings were from the Ephesians and from the rest of the assemblies throughout the province of Asia Minor.

He also included a greeting from Priscilla and Aquila, as they had lived in Corinth for such a long time, and the church there loved them dearly.

Here are Paul's closing thoughts:

> The churches here in the province of Asia greet you heartily in the Lord, along with Aquila and Priscilla and all the others who gather in their home for church meetings. All the brothers and sisters here have asked me to greet you for them. Greet each other in Christian love.

(Perhaps Paul was reminding Corinth that when Paul, the six young brothers, and Priscilla and Aquila arrived in Ephesus, there was only one church in that province. Now, at the end of those years, there were several more.) Paul stepped out of the room. It seemed Priscilla needed to tell him something important. In a moment Paul was back in the room.

Paul motioned for me to hand him the pen and paper. As he looked at the parchment he squinted his eyes, leaned closer to the torch that lighted the room, and wrote in a huge scrawl:

> Here is my greeting, which I write with my own hand—PAUL.

He handed the letter back for me to write one last word:

> If anyone does not love the Lord, that person is cursed. Our Lord, come! May the grace of the Lord Jesus be with you. My love to all of you in Christ Jesus.

So ended a long day. Paul had poured out his heart to a church that so often broke his heart, yet so often gave him joy.

It was now a matter of getting the letter to Corinth, or so Paul thought. But what happened almost immediately thereafter changed everything.

(The riot was only days away.)

News that followers of Blastinius had arrived in Corinth would stun Paul! So also the news that the Daggermen were on their way to Greece to find Paul and kill him. Because of all this, Paul changed his plans. A few days after Sosthenes departed with the letter, Titus, not Timothy, would make the trip to Corinth, observe the conditions of the church, and then report back to Paul.

When Paul told Titus of this change in plans, Titus protested mightily: "I have never been in Greece. I know nothing of life in Greece."

"You are refusing?" asked Paul.

"Why no. But I quote Timothy when you sent him to Thessalonica: 'If I fail, is it your fault, not mine?' "

The simple act of Titus's journeying from Ephesus to Corinth turned out to cause the worst, most traumatic hour of Paul's life. The reason? After Titus left Corinth on his way back to Paul, Titus disappeared. All evidence indicated that Titus had fallen victim to the Daggermen.

But all that was future.

At the moment all attention was on Titus's going to Corinth and Priscilla and Aquila to Rome!

Having finished the letter to Corinth, Paul announced that there would be a very important meeting the next day at the school of Tyrranus. "Priscilla has shared with me some earth-shaking news."

CHAPTER 30

Priscilla has bought a house in Rome. And, as hoped, it is located on Aventine Hill."

"She bought it without ever seeing it?" asked Gaius.

"On the contrary, she *has* seen it! She is familiar with this house. She has often been a guest there. That is what is making it so easy to negotiate its purchase," explained Paul. "Priscilla tells me that it is ideally located and a perfect place for the assembly to gather.

"Priscilla and Aquila will be leaving Ephesus, bound for Rome, very soon. As of today I will be writing a letter to all the Gentile churches, asking each church to send someone to Rome immediately. Priscilla has already written clear instructions as to how to find the house upon arriving in Rome. At last, everything is in place. Gentile Christians are headed for Rome! There will yet be a Gentile expression of the ecclesia in that Gentile city."

"How many do you expect to leave their churches and go to Rome?"

Paul paused and began counting, then looked up, his eyes bright.

"At *least* thirty!"

We broke out into cheers.

"I need to tell you that we will soon be giving up Tyrannus's school. I have notified him. Our time in Ephesus is drawing to an end.

"As you know, I have written a letter to Corinth. Sosthenes will take the letter. Titus will go shortly thereafter.

"It has been six years since I first entered Corinth. Upon arriving there I wrote a letter to Thessalonica. In that letter I addressed the problems that the Thessalonians were having. Six years have passed. This time I have been forced to write to Corinth. Many of the problems there are serious, a few quite grave.

"I have faced no problem of this magnitude in any of the churches since the day Blastinius invaded Galatia."

Titus interrupted, "I want everyone to know what I told Paul. If the church in Corinth disintegrates, I will forever believe it was my fault. But I intend to place the blame on Paul for using such poor judgment in choosing me."

Paul threw Titus's own words back at him. "Titus of Antioch, you will go to Corinth. You are qualified, and you will minister. And minister. And minister. And it will be the Lord Jesus Christ whom you minister to these people."

"Oh no," Titus groaned, as he put his hands to his face, "I have been wounded by my own spear."

"You should not have given me the reply that you did, Titus. But when you did, you won for yourself a follow-up on the Corinthian letter. When you arrive in Corinth you will minister to an assembly that is in great need of hearing more about the Lord Jesus Christ."

The optimism displayed by Paul that day masked the pain in his heart. Nonetheless, there was true joy in that room, as hope for Corinth came alive.

What we did not know was that Paul had only begun to surprise us. We were all about to receive the news of our lives.

CHAPTER 31

"Not only are Priscilla and Aquila going to Rome, so are others. And there's more to tell," announced Paul.

"I sense that our time here in Ephesus is almost over. In perhaps no more than two or three months we may all be leaving. When we leave, I want all eight of you to go with me as I visit the young churches that have sprung up here in Asia Minor—all of them. After all, these are the churches that *you* brothers have raised up.

"After that, we will leave Asia Minor and visit the churches in Greece, Galatia, and Cilicia. And Syria. Along the way we will be gathering money from the churches, which *we* shall carry to the poor in Jerusalem."

"What?" cried Gaius.

Paul smiled.

"Did you say *we?*"

"Yes . . . we! Every one of you men will go with me to all these places; *then* you will *all* accompany me to Jerusalem."

Suddenly eight men were on their feet, cheering, shouting, and hugging one another.

When at last we settled down, Paul *tried* to look a little exasperated with us. Nonetheless, the pride he was feeling was clearly showing through.

"The money coming from Asia Minor will be placed in the hands of Tychicus and Trophimus. The money that comes from Galatia will be put in the hands of Gaius. The money coming from Greece will be carried by the hands of Aristarchus, Sopater, and Secundus. The money from Syria and Cilicia will be in the hands of . . . " Paul paused. "Titus . . . "

Then Paul added a word that once more surprised us. " . . . and Luke."

We were being told too many things, too quickly. We were struggling to grasp the moment.

"I have just received word that Luke is on his way here to Ephesus. He is bringing news. What the news is I do not know, but I can tell you now, it will not be good. Twice before Luke has come to me from Antioch. And twice before the news he has brought has been disturbing."

There was a moment of silence, then Tychicus broke it. "Paul, let us go back to that part about Jerusalem. Do you mean *all* eight of us are going to *Jerusalem?*"

"Yes, *all* eight of you. You will serve as messengers from the churches in Greece, Asia Minor, Galatia, Cilicia, and Syria. You will count the money when the churches hand it to you. You will then count the money in the presence of the church in Jerusalem. Then you will testify whether or not the amount that you were given is the amount that you are giving to the Jerusalem church."

Then Paul broke into a broad smile. "I will personally take you brothers around the city of Jerusalem and tell you everything I know."

Paul was savoring every word.

Instantly we surrounded Paul and began hugging him—and one another, not to mention making a great deal of jubilant noise.

After we calmed down, Paul continued.

"I have always felt it important that you *eight* meet the *Twelve.*"

"The Twelve?" burst out Gaius. "The Twelve!"

"Yes, the Twelve. Further, it is important that you see Jerusalem. But most of all, I want the brothers and sisters in Jerusalem to see that there *are* Gentile *workers!* I desire that they get to know you. I feel certain within my spirit that the day will come when many of the Hebrews will be fleeing Israel. In that day many *believing* Jews will be coming to Gentile countries. Countries which you brothers represent."

Paul ran his fingers through his hair.

"I am not sure that I should say these things to you. *Do not let my words leave this room. This* must be kept secret! There are many Jewish Christians, all over the empire, who are very offended at what is happening in Jerusalem: The unbelieving Jews are being very unfair to the believing poor. The crops are terrible. Many need food. There is money being sent by Jews to the Jerusalem Temple from all over the world. Traditionally, this money is sent as a Jewish tax to sustain the Temple and care for the poor. Except they are not helping the poor who are believers!

"Here is the part that I desire you tell no one: Among the Jews in the Gentile churches, and on Cyprus and in Syria, the Jewish brothers and sisters are *not* sending their taxes to the Temple. They are holding back their tax money to send directly to the poor believers in Israel—the ones who are being neglected by the rulers of the Temple.

"It is *that* money that we will be carrying with us to Jerusalem. The amount we bring to Jerusalem is not small. I thank God that both the Jews and the Gentiles are working together in doing this.

"But mark my words . . . there will be repercussions. Terrible repercussions."

As I, Timothy, sat there realizing all the burdens now pressing down on Paul, I could not help but think, *All these crises—enough to crush ten men, and now here is yet another for Paul to carry.*

"About Corinth and the letter to them," said Paul, changing the subject abruptly. "You have been going out to the towns and villages around Ephesus. You have experienced the life of the church here in this city—you know church life. You know a little about your Lord . . . and now I wish to acquaint you with the real situation in Corinth. The believers there face more problems than all the other churches combined.

"We are going to pray that God delivers Corinth out of this crisis . . . then . . . then we will step back and trust, and rest, and see what God does!"

Paul then shared his deepest fears about the Corinthian crucible.

We knelt and began to pray. For a long time we poured out our hearts before the Lord. That day Corinth was well prayed for.

Paul closed with these words: "Just before Titus leaves, he will read a copy of the Corinthian letter to you."

A few days later Apollos arrived in Ephesus. He had come from Greece to speak to Paul about Corinth, and—as far as he was capable—to apologize to Paul for the trouble he had created in Corinth.

Apollos's presence caused Paul to consider tearing up the Corinthian letter. (Apollos knew nothing of the existence of Paul's letter.)

Paul graciously asked Apollos to return to Corinth to minister there again. Apollos adamantly refused. With that, Paul continued with his plans to send the letter on to Corinth.

Shortly thereafter Paul called us together in Tyrannus's school. We all knew why.

Eight men were about to hear Paul's letter.

CHAPTER 32

It was late afternoon.

Paul asked us to sit down, then unrolled the parchment and handed it to Titus to read. Six men noted that the letter was long—very long. A lump formed in my throat. I had not realized that, even though I had transcribed the letter, what Paul said could destroy the church or at least bring it to a massive crisis. It was clear to us all that Paul was risking the existence of the church in Corinth.

But Paul, in risking the existence of the church, had also surrendered the existence of that church to the Lord.

I, Timothy, look back and remember how many men have fought—and fought without scruples—to preserve their work . . . not caring whom they hurt nor what cruel things they said. They fought! Fought to keep *their* ministry. That others were criticized, blamed, and destroyed was not important. That their conduct caused great damage was immaterial. Survival of the work was *everything*.

Not so with Paul. Before he wrote the Corinthian letter, Paul had brought the church in Corinth before the throne of God and there, after great struggle, had surrendered her to the Lord. The destiny of the church in Corinth was, from that moment on, in the hands of a sovereign God.

When Titus finished reading the copy of the letter, we prayed again.

Just three days later Sosthenes bought passage on a ship bound for Cenchrea, Greece. During those three days the entire church spent much time in praying for him and for Corinth. And we knew that every one of those prayers was needed!

One week later Titus sailed for Corinth. The night before his ship was scheduled to depart from Ephesus, Gaius and I awoke Titus. We had a surprise for him.

CHAPTER 33

"Come!" said Gaius.

As Titus came out of his room, I motioned for him to follow me to the front door. Titus, thinking that there was some last word the two brothers wanted to share with him, followed.

He innocently stepped out into the night. There in the street stood six young men waiting for him.

"Surprise!" said Gaius.

"What are you all doing here?"

"What are we doing here—we are standing here in the middle of the street envying you; *that* is what we are doing."

"I wish I could go with you," said Tychicus.

"I do not," said Trophimus. "I wish Titus were not even going and that I was going!"

"Well then, I will tell you something to make you even more envious," Titus rejoined. "I happen to know that in a few weeks Timothy will be going to northern Greece."

Everyone groaned, now envious of the two of us.

"Do not be too jealous," Titus continued. "When he gets there, he is probably going to have to confront the Judaizers. There is a party of them on their way to Macedonia right now."

That immediately sobered everyone.

"Then I do not envy you at all," answered Aristarchus. "Macedonia is my home, and I know how we greet visitors. With open arms."

"You brothers should be in bed," said Titus, feigning anger.

"We have come to be with you on your last night in Ephesus, and what is more, we have another surprise for you."

At that moment out of one of the nearby doorways stepped a tall figure. Titus immediately recognized the silhouette.

"Epaphras!" he cried, overwhelmed with joy.

We hugged, we shouted, we praised the Lord. We made spectacles of ourselves—*that* is what we did all night, enjoying every moment of it.

We nine euphoric brothers wandered the streets of Ephesus, shouting and praising and singing at the top of our voices. It was good, so very good, to have Epaphras with us again. We had always considered him to be one of us. It was for that reason we had written to Epaphras (in Colosse) asking him to come to Ephesus before Titus left for Corinth. He had managed to arrive just hours before Titus's ship sailed.

Arm in arm we walked the city streets. Occasionally one of these deranged young men would cry out, "Jesus Christ is Lord of Ephesus!" which was always followed by shouts and cheers.

Once, we found ourselves in front of the Jewish synagogue. (It is in the northern part of the city.) We stood before this building thanking God that Paul had been allowed to speak there for three entire months. We then offered up to our Lord the names of those in the synagogue who were still considering Christ.

From the synagogue we walked out of the city to the Cayster River. There we knelt down in the very place where twelve followers of John received Jesus Christ as their Lord. We prayed for Epenetus, one of those baptized that day, who was now about to go to Rome with Priscilla and Aquila.

Then we prayed for Epaphras and for his city of Colosse,

for he, too, had been baptized in the Cayster River. He then asked us to pray for Hieropolis and Laodicea, for he was determined to take Christ to those two cities . . . which were so near Colosse.

There along the riverbank we knelt with our faces to the ground before God, asking him to never allow us to be men who would be cruel to God's people . . . that we would never fight to maintain our work. We asked him that any work we did would be able to stand in the presence of the onslaught of our detractors and any critics. We asked God to so direct our lives that we would build only with gold and silver and costly stone.

We then walked back to Ephesus and into the Roman agora. There we prayed that, after we departed Ephesus, God would raise up young men who spoke Latin to proclaim Christ to the Italians who shopped there every day. And for those same men to take Christ to the entire Latin world.

I remember one brother praying, "Lord, save an Italian in Rome, and then send him here to Ephesus to preach in the Latin market! Save a man in Greece, and send him here to proclaim *you* in the other marketplace—the Greek market."

We then prayed for all those brothers and sisters in the Gentile churches all over the empire who were, even at that moment, preparing to leave their houses to travel to Rome. We prayed for Priscilla and Aquila, for their new home on Aventine Hill, and for that very first meeting soon to take place in their living room.

As we walked along we continued praying for the young assemblies recently raised up in Thyatira, Sardis, Smyrna, Magnesia, and all places where we had preached the gospel and had seen men saved.

We turned our prayer toward Philadelphia, for we had just received a letter from brothers in that city asking that someone come and help a little band of believers there who had just begun to assemble.

We prayed that strong assemblies would come from each of these cities, for we very much loved the brothers and sisters in every one of those places. As we prayed, we lost complete control of ourselves. We began to cry. Soon all we could offer was our sobs.

As men, we confessed how weak, incapable, and afraid we were. We asked our God to make us broken men. Broken in spirit. We asked him to own our wills, especially where it came to the life of the churches.

Soon nine men were praying for Paul. We prayed for his failing health. We asked the Lord to keep him safe from the Daggermen, to give him a safe journey to Jerusalem, and to allow Paul his dream: *Rome!*

"Lord, you gave him one of his dreams—Ephesus! And eight men . . . no, *nine*. . . to take his place when he dies. Before he dies, let him proclaim *you* in Rome! Let him have his *Rome!*"

You cannot imagine some of the prayers nine young men prayed that night. Nor would we have even dared tell you some of the things we said to the Lord that night of nights. The longer we prayed, the wilder our prayers became. Whether God has answered all these prayers, I, Timothy, do not know. Whether he will someday answer them all, I do not know. But I thank God for every word we offered to him. That night changed our souls forever!

Gaius began asking the Lord to keep us safe all the way to Jerusalem so that we might be able to meet the Twelve and to sit at their feet. Suddenly our prayers turned. We began praying for the Gentile world—*our world*—the heathen world. We begged our God that we be found as faithful to Christ and the Gentile world as the Twelve had been in the world of the Jews. Have any young men ever prayed so?

(Even now, as we nine men depart this stage—just as the Twelve have all already departed, except John—I pray to God this day that he will raise up a new generation of men to take *our* places.)

We stood, we wiped our tears, we hugged. We thanked the Lord for giving us the privilege of sitting at the feet of Paul of Tarsus. Perhaps *that* is when we wept the most.

I thought we were going back to Priscilla's house because, after all, dawn was not far away. Then someone—I think it was that insane brother Gaius—suggested that we go up to the temple of Artemis!

And so there on an Ephesian night, we set out for one of the seven wonders of the world. Arriving at the temple, we saw the torches' reflection on the beautiful polished marble. Secundus mounted the very first temple step and began to speak to the temple.

"You were built three hundred years ago. An earthquake brought you down and destroyed you, but you were rebuilt. Earthquakes can bring you down again. May the Lord one day level you forever."

Secundus continued, "You are called a place of refuge—many come inside your walls to keep from being arrested. There is a better refuge than you, temple of Artemis—the greatest refuge of all, Jesus Christ."

Arm in arm, we walked up all fourteen steps and stared at the curious figures that had been carved on some of the stone pillars. Then quite out of our minds, we walked between the double rows of the fluted pillars. As we marched we began speaking to our Lord.

Someone again—I think it was Gaius—announced, "You may each weigh thirty thousand pounds, but one day the Lord will bring every one of you crashing down."

We marched as far into the temple as is allowed—that is, to the pillars of green jasper and the curtain surrounding the idol.

Our presence did not go unnoticed. Some of the eunuch priests of the order of Megabyzi began to follow us around. Later, some of the priests of the order of Curetes came out and stared at us. We didn't care!

Eventually, having prayed for the destruction of that temple in every way we could think of, we left, singing an ode to Jesus Christ. Just as we departed, one of the priests of the order of Acrobatae came out, looked at us, shrugged his shoulders contemptuously, and snarled, "Christians!"

Passing back into the city, this time through the Mithradates Gate, we emerged onto the street called Marble. This time we walked to the Dorcices Market. We sat there together until the first rays of morning streamed across the eastern hills. Then we did one last thing. We marched out to the amphitheater, sat down on the stage, and began to sing and call forth the dawn.

(None of us could have imagined that only a few days later the largest riot in the history of Ephesus would take place in that very amphitheater . . . and it would all be because of *Paul.*)

For the third time that night, our arms locked around one another's shoulders, we marched back into the city. We brothers then led Titus back to his room and ordered him to bed.

"We will go down to Port Coressus and wait until your ship is almost ready to sail. Then we will come back and awaken you."

Ships are always scheduled to leave at dawn but rarely ever do. It was almost noon when the brothers came and awakened Titus. He was not allowed to pick up so much as a single bag. Eight other brothers fought one another for that privilege. (One bag was so full of food it would have been found worthy of being carried by John Mark. Two of us carried it.)

As we walked toward the docks, Titus turned and took one last look at the water clock that hangs in the center of the

Hellenic market. Then, for the last time, he passed out of Ephesus by way of the Harbor Gate. From there we turned west on the main road—the very road by which we had entered Ephesus three years earlier.

From the direction of the harbor we heard singing. There on the docks we found over a hundred brothers and sisters waiting to see Titus off. Among them was his uncle Luke, who never seemed to really believe all these things were happening to his earnest nephew.

Paul stepped out from the crowd. "Are you ready?"

"As ready as Timothy was the day you sent him to Thessalonica."

"May the riches and grace of Jesus Christ go with you and in great abundance," said Paul as he embraced Titus.

"Now listen to me, carefully. Timothy will soon be going to Philippi. From there he will go down to Thessalonica and then to Berea. After that he will travel back up to Philippi. During all this time *you*, Titus, will be in Corinth. I have told Timothy not to leave Philippi until you join him there. So, while in Corinth, stay in contact with him so that he will know when you are ready to leave Corinth for Philippi. Write Timothy often—if at all possible, by courier. Spare no expense to contact him. Timothy, in turn, will stay in contact with me.

"I have waited as long as possible before sending Timothy to the churches of Macedonia. I have done this so that Blastinius may have all the time he needs to do his mischief in Philippi and Thessalonica. By now, Blastinius *is* in Philippi. Either that or he has sent others like him.

"Remember, Timothy will wait for you in Philippi. When you leave Corinth, go nowhere except to Philippi."

Then, putting his hand on Titus's shoulder, Paul added, "Titus, it is imperative for me to know if the church in Corinth still exists! I will not draw an easy breath until I know the answer. By now Corinth has read the letter. Go . . . remain . . . help. Then, when you are sure of the reaction, whatever that may be, go immediately to Philippi. Report to Timothy everything that has happened to you in Corinth. If the Corinthian church is still in existence, if the gathering is capable of receiving a guest . . . if the Corinthians are well, then send Timothy to collect the money that the brothers and sisters in Corinth have set aside for the poor in Jerusalem. At that very same time you *must* leave Philippi and come to meet me in Troas."

"Soon I leave Ephesus and go to Troas. There is a wide door that has opened for me in Troas. The Jews who lead the synagogue there want me to come and make Christians of them! I must pass through that door.

"Titus, when I see you—" Paul's eyes filled with tears—"I will have but one question: Is there an ecclesia in Corinth? If so, I will have a second question, which is just as important: Am I still welcomed in Corinth?"

"I will do as you say. And be assured, you will find me when you arrive in Troas."

"Troas has resisted the best efforts of Blastinius and his friends. Many Gentiles in Troas have also turned to the Lord. We will see those marvels together." Paul's voice cracked. "Come to me in Troas as quickly as you can. My heart is breaking."

"These are dark days for you, brother Paul. Corinth, Apollos, the Daggermen. And Peter now in as much danger as you. The unrest in Israel. And Blastinius, always Blastinius. And now, a letter to a church that may destroy that church."

Paul's eyes looked out to the sea. "Yes, Titus, these are among the darkest days of all."

"I hope to brighten one small place in your life when I see you in Troas. I hope to bring you good news from Corinth."

Someone called out, "It is time!"

The slaves had moved to the sides of the ship and made

ready to push the ship into the sea. I, Timothy, felt a cold chill come over me.

Titus embraced Paul one last time.

The brothers and sisters all gathered around Titus and sang one final song of farewell. Eight brothers walked with Titus up the gangplank. Together, we grabbed Titus and held on to him furiously, while we all wept.

The captain ordered the brothers off the ship. Titus gave Epaphras one last hug. The ship began to move along the edge of the pier and out into the Ephesian Gulf.

Titus turned to look back at Ephesus, then heard Paul call out, "Meet me in Troas. Do not forget to meet me in Troas!"

Titus, his eyes filled with tears, called back, "I will, but remember, I am unworthy of this task."

The last thing I remember seeing was Paul of Tarsus standing on the pier, waving to a young man from Antioch, Syria, who had absolutely no business doing what he was doing—just as I once had no business going to Thessalonica.

Still, everything in me knew Titus would do beautifully in Corinth. After all, he had managed greater crises. Years ago in Jerusalem, this uncircumcised Syrian had stood up to the Twelve.

CHAPTER 34

Some thirty or more Gentiles, from churches all over the empire, were on their way to Ephesus to journey with Priscilla and Aquila to Rome. Most had managed to plan their route through Ephesus!

A few weeks after that, there was a riot in the city. That riot signaled to Paul that it was time for him to leave Ephesus. The day he left he had to play cat and mouse with the Daggermen, who had arrived in the city to kill him.

Blastinius was in northern Greece doing everything he could to stir up trouble both in the churches and in the synagogues as well as among the civil authorities.

There was a famine in Israel.

There was growing tension between the Gentile churches and the Jewish churches. (If there was a rupture between the churches, the very work of God on this earth would be in jeopardy.)

Priscilla and Aquila were in danger of having their heads chopped off in Rome.

I, Timothy, was about to leave Paul's company, almost certain to face Blastinius in Philippi.

But in all this the Lord had a crushing burden to place upon

Paul that was more unendurable than all the others combined. He would flee Ephesus by taking a circuitous route to keep from being killed by those who vowed to murder him or die trying. Upon arriving in Troas, Paul would discover Titus was *not there.* Had Titus been murdered? Paul was so burdened it almost destroyed him, causing him to later confess, "I despaired of life!"

Paul truly thought Titus had been killed, in *his* place.

Before we learn what happened in Troas, we must first learn of the Ephesian riot. And also of Priscilla and Aquila's journey to Rome.

I have requested that Lady Priscilla continue the story from this point on. She, better than anyone, can tell you of Paul's arrival in Rome and his subsequent death.

EPILOGUE

I am Priscilla of Rome.

News has just come to me that Timothy is in hiding. The emperor Nero has marked Timothy for death.

Nonetheless, a letter from Timothy has reached me here in Rome. As you know, Timothy has recounted for us Paul's third journey—his journey to Ephesus. In his letter to me, Timothy has asked that I continue the story. Therefore, beginning today, I will attempt to continue the story that Silas, Titus, and Timothy began.

Timothy was correct in mentioning the many crises Paul would face immediately after he wrote his first letter to Corinth. There was a riot in Ephesus, then the disappearance of Titus, the arrival of Blastinius in Corinth, and a serious possibility of a breach in unity between the Jewish churches and the Gentile churches.

While all those crises were taking place, my husband, Aquila, and I were facing the distinct possibility of being beheaded for reentering Rome. (My husband is Jewish . . . and the decree banishing Jews was still in effect when we arrived in Rome.)

All of this fell hard on Paul. During this time he was a very distraught man—that is, until he found Titus *alive.*

I will attempt to tell you of all these things, as well as Paul's second letter to Corinth, his wonderful letter to Rome, his journey from Corinth to Jerusalem, and the riot in Jerusalem, which almost cost Paul his life. Then, finally, Paul's imprisonment in Caesarea . . . as well as his harrowing voyage to Rome.

—Priscilla of Rome

Priscilla's DIARY

You are there at the largest riot ever seen in Ephesus. And Paul caused it! Be there as Paul and a group of young men make their way to Jerusalem, dodging the Daggermen all the way, only to see Paul almost torn to pieces in yet another riot.

Journey with Paul on his way to Rome as a prisoner, when he experiences his fourth—and worst—shipwreck.

Listen as Priscilla tells you about Rome, Nero, and how she was almost beheaded for being in Rome at the wrong time. Do not miss *Priscilla's Diary*, the fourth of the First-Century Diaries.

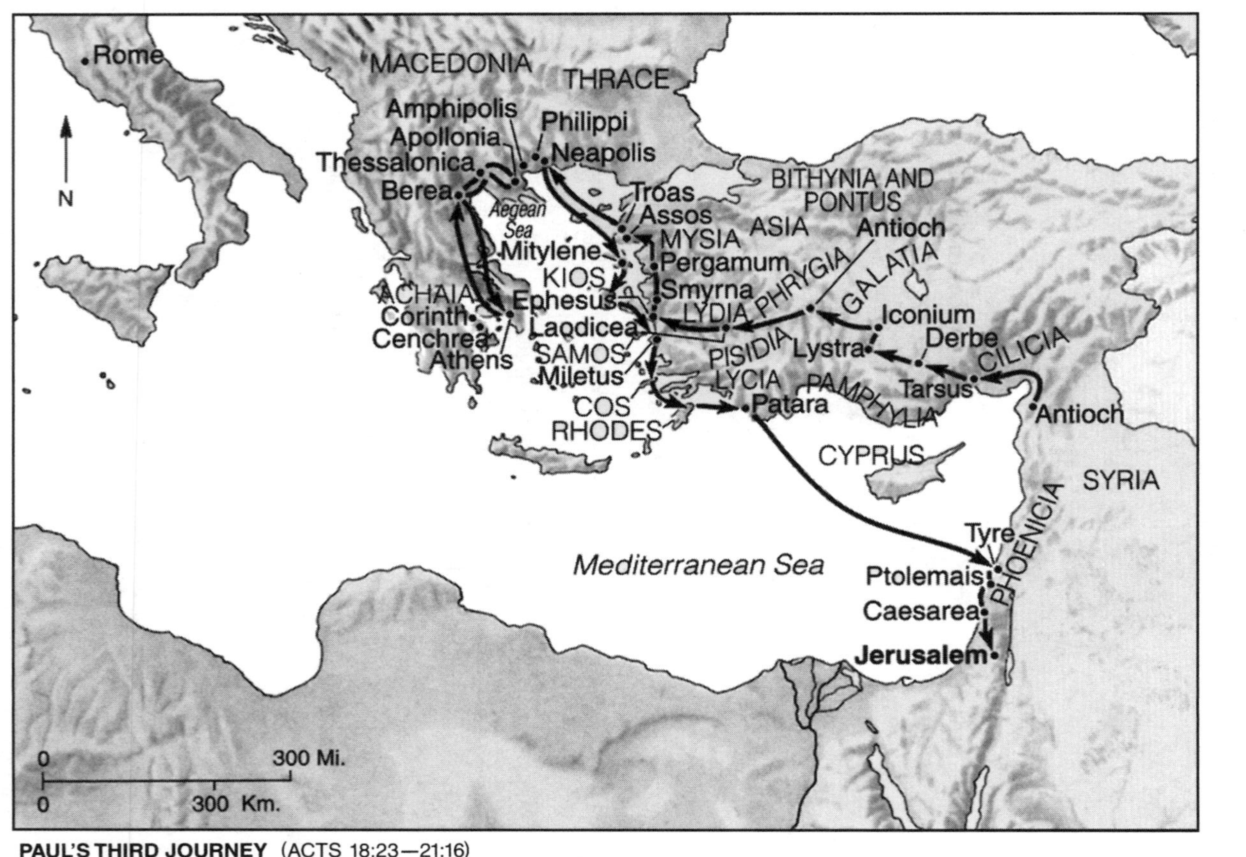

PAUL'S THIRD JOURNEY (ACTS 18:23—21:16)

FREE!

If you would like to receive a free copy of *Revolution*, a book that covers the first seventeen years of the Christian story, write to the author at:

Gene Edwards' Ministry
P.O. Box 3317
Jacksonville, FL 32206
800-228-2665

Since the Protestant Reformation there have risen only a few men who write, speak, and minister in ways unlike the generation in which they live. Edwards has proven to be one of those original thinkers.

To read Gene Edwards is to walk into new dimensions of the Christian faith. His books are always a surprise. His writings contain nothing similar to contemporary authors, nor to the generation that came before. His books have become literary classics...never-out-of-date...never out-of-style...and remaining always popular.

The Divine Romance and *A Tale of Three Kings* have been classed as among the best Christian literature since the Elizabethan age.

Beyond this, Edwards has pioneered the house church movement in America, bringing forth a whole new dimension as to what *ecclesia* means and how it functions. He has been called the dean of the house church movement. You will want to read his *First-Century Diaries* and *How to Meet in Homes.*

Edwards graduated from college at the age of 18 and then tromped the entire Holy Lands and lived in Rome before the age of 20 and then finished seminary at age 22.

SeedSowers

P.O. Box 3317, Jacksonville, FL 32206
800-228-2665
904-598-3456 (fax) www.seedsowers.com

Revolutionary books on Church

How to Meet In Homes (*Edwards*) 10.95
An Open Letter to House Church Leaders (*Edwards*) 4.00
When the Church Was Led Only by Laymen *(Edwards)* 4.00
Beyond Radical (*Edwards*) 5.95
Rethinking Elders (*Edwards*) 9.95
Revolution, The Story of the Early Church (*Edwards*) 8.95
The Silas Diary (*Edwards*) 9.99
The Titus Diary (*Edwards*) 8.99
The Timothy Diary (*Edwards*) 9.99
The Priscilla Diary (*Edwards*) 9.99
The Gaius Diary *(Edwards)* 10.99
Overlooked Christianity (*Edwards*) 14.95

An introduction to the deeper Christian life

Living by the Highest Life (*Edwards*) 8.99
The Secret to the Christian Life (*Edwards*) 8.99
The Inward Journey (*Edwards*) 8.99

Classics on the deeper Christian life

Experiencing the Depths of Jesus Christ (*Guyon*) 8.95
Practicing His Presence (*Lawrence Laubach*) 8.95
The Spiritual Guide (*Molinos*) 8.95
Union With God (*Guyon*) 8.95
The Seeking Heart (*Fenelon*) 9.95
Intimacy with Christ (*Guyon*) 10.95
The Song of the Bride *(Guyon)* 9.95
Spiritual Torrents (*Guyon*) 10.95
The Ultimate Intention (*Fromke*) 11.00

In a class by themselves

The Divine Romance (*Edwards*) 8.95
The Story of My Life as told by Jesus Christ *(Four gospels blended)* 14.95
Acts in First Person *(Book of Acts)* 9.95

Commentaries by Jeanne Guyon

Genesis Commentary 10.95
Exodus Commentary 10.95
Leviticus - Numbers - Deuteronomy Commentaries 14.95
Judges Commentary 7.95
Job Commentary 10.95
Song of Songs *(Song of Solomon Commentary)* 9.95
Jeremiah Commentary 7.95
James - I John - Revelation Commentaries 14.95